BETSY ZANE

the Rose of Fort Henry

Also by LYNDA DURRANT

Echohawk
The Beaded Moccasins
Turtle Clan Journey

BETSY ZANE
the Rose of Fort Henry

LYNDA DURRANT

Clarion Books • New York

Clarion Books
a Houghton Mifflin Company imprint
215 Park Avenue South, New York, NY 10003

The text was set in 13.5-point Centaur.

www.hmco.com/trade

Printed in the USA.

Library of Congress Cataloging-in-Publication Data

Durrant, Lynda, 1956–
Betsy Zane, the rose of Fort Henry / by Lynda Durrant.
p.   cm.
Summary: In 1781 twelve-year-old Elizabeth Zane, great-great-aunt of novelist Zane Grey,
leaves Philadelphia to return to her brothers' homestead near Fort Henry in what is now West Virginia,
where she plays an important role in the final battle of the American Revolution.
ISBN 0-395-97899-8
I. Zane, Elizabeth 1769–1823—Juvenile fiction. [I. Zane, Elizabeth,
1769–1823—Fiction. 2. Fort Henry (W. Va.)—Fiction.
3. United States—History—Revolution, 1775–1883—Fiction.] I. Title.

PZ7.D93428 Ro 2000
[Fic]—dc21
00-026027

HAD 10 9 8 7 6 5 4 3

To Starr and Sara, our own Betsy Zanes

Contents

1   August, 1781   1

2   Escape   16

3   Secrets   30

4   Buffalo Roads   46

5   The Ohio   62

6   The Zanes   76

7   Myeerah   81

8   *Juledag*   97

9   Lost in the Hay   113

10   The War   128

11   The Colonels   143

12   Vengeance   157

13   The Apron   171

14   October Roses   184

   AFTERWORD   189

   SOURCES   197

1

August, 1781

Look, Betsy, there's Zane Street, named after your great-great-grandfather Karl Zane. He was one of the founders of Philadelphia, with none other than William Penn himself."

Great-Aunt Elizabeth turns in her carriage seat and points grandly down Zane Street, which is really not much more than an alley. So narrow is Zane Street that I could stand in the middle of it and almost touch the one-room shacks on either side, which in turn are as jammed together as pickled herring in a crockery jar.

Not that I'd want to stand in Zane Street. The garbage and animal droppings are knee deep. People, pigs, dogs, cows, and goats pick their way through the steaming filth. The heat this morning is fierce, the flies fiercer still.

"Yes, Great-Aunt Elizabeth," I say in what I hope is a patient voice. "I know all about Zane Street, and Karl Zane, and William Penn. We Zanes have lived in Philadelphia since 1680."

We Zanes who remain here—just Great-Aunt Elizabeth and I—live on a side street off Third and Market called Church Street.

Behind our house and stable is Christ Church. Great-Aunt Elizabeth watched the new Christ Church being built in 1754. She had been a babe-in-arms when the first Christ Church was built in 1695.

Monday is market day in the Zane household. After breakfast Young Sam hitches Maybelle to our carriage and I drive. Instead of turning toward the Delaware River and the High Street Market, I am obliged to go roundabout past Zane Street, just so Great-Aunt Elizabeth can tell me about it (and us) all over again.

She replies in a peevish voice, "My, my aren't you a clever girl, Miss Elizabeth Zane. Soon there will be no reason to listen to an old woman at all. You will know as much as Benjamin Franklin, Thomas Jefferson, and King George, all rolled into one."

"King George is as mad as a loon and you shouldn't praise him, not even in jest," I whisper, turning right onto Arch Street. Perchance it's my imagination, but the air seems a bit fresher already as we head east toward the river. "There are spies afoot."

"Spies!" She snorts. "Who'd heed the ranting of an old woman when even her own great-niece—her own namesake!—won't listen to her? When I was a girl, young folks had manners."

"I listen to you, Great-Aunt Elizabeth."

And how could I not? For she is always talking. Everything she sees reminds her of a story about something else.

Unlike Zane Street, most of the streets in Philadelphia

are cobblestoned. I've been told that not even London has as many paved streets. But we don't get to admire these cobblestones often. Pigs have our aldermen's leave to run free. Unless the pigs are hungry, the garbage piles up hip deep.

In front of Betsy Ross Ashbourne's house our old mare pulls our carriage over a pile of moldy manure the size of a footstool. Mrs. Ashbourne's many children are in the courtyard. They wave, and we wave back.

Driving past Zane Street every Monday doesn't cheer me. It reminds me of where the Zanes have been, and I want to be where the Zanes are now.

My brothers—Ebenezer, Andrew, Jonathan, Silas, and (I hope) Isaac—are on the cool, green Virginia shore of the Ohio River. They live in the Virginia Zane House, in a settlement we named Zane Station. Our father named the nearby fortress Fort Henry, after a fiery orator from Virginia, Patrick Henry. When I was small, I lived there, too.

My memories of Zane Station are lodged in my mind like burrs stuck to a horse's forelock. In my mind's eye I see sprawling Zane House, made of logs and spread out on a cliff overlooking the Ohio. My father and brothers built rooms on the river side for the officers and soldiers, before Fort Henry was built. Those rooms are now the kitchen, a sitting room, and, with the north wall removed, the river porch. I can still smell the sweet, pure air scented with balsam and locust blossom. I can still feel the Ohio River mud creeping between my toes.

I remember standing on the river porch one day with Jonathan when I was six. We gazed across to the Ohio shore.

"Have a good look, Betsy," he said. He hoisted me up on his shoulders. It was high summer, and the foliage across the river was as thick as one of Fort Henry's ramparts.

"Someday, Betsy," Jonathan said proudly, "someday the Zanes will return to the Ohio country in style."

I knew, even then, that he didn't mean returning as captives. All my brothers had been held captive, some of them for years, by either the Delaware or the Wyandot. Our parents had been obliged to go to Fort Detroit and pay a pretty penny to ransom them home.

He meant that someday that wild country would be ours.

"Will they name it after us, Jonathan?" I had asked.

Jonathan had chuckled. "Zanesylvania? They might. Although 'Ohio' sounds prettier, doesn't it?"

But then, when I was seven, our parents were killed by Indians. My eldest brother, Ebenezer, said to me, "The wilderness is no place for a little girl to live without her mother. Henceforth, you shall live in the Philadelphia Zane House. I can only hope that Great-Aunt Elizabeth will teach you to become a lady."

I was sent to Great-Aunt Elizabeth's, to live on Church Street. For six years now, the wilderness of my birth has been nothing but a memory.

"The cool, green Virginia shore," I mutter to myself.

"What?" Great-Aunt Elizabeth shouts in her cracking voice.

"Nothing."

Our old mare pulls up beside High Street Market. I jump out of the driver's box, run round to the other side, and help Great-Aunt Elizabeth down. We sink to our ankles in mud as hot and sticky as this morning's porridge.

High Street Market is a narrow alley between Second and Front Streets, next to Elfreth's Alley. This August morning the High Street Market is airless, jammed with people, and as hot as a blacksmith's forge. The cobblestones are crowded with carriages, shoppers, chickens squawking in crates, herds of pigs and goats, beggars, pickpockets, and men in tattered army uniforms.

Some Mondays we stop in one of the many coffee and chocolate houses along Penn's Landing. It's exciting watching the ships—from Halifax, Boston, Nantucket, Providence, New York, Baltimore, Charleston, Savannah—sail up the Delaware River. Before the war we'd also see merchant ships from London, Bristol, Liverpool, Belfast, even from Barbados in the West Indies.

The ships remind me that Philadelphia is a seaport, even though the Atlantic is a hundred miles away.

But this morning it's too hot for coffee.

I drape the quilts over my arm. I pull a cologne-drenched handkerchief out of my sleeve and push through the crowds, towing Great-Aunt Elizabeth behind me.

With one hand holding the quilts against me, and the other pulling my great-aunt along, I don't have a free hand to hold my handkerchief to my nose. The heat and stench make me muzzy headed.

"Betsy, look!"

My great-aunt points to a man playing "Yankee Doodle" on a fife. Two dogs, standing on their back legs and wearing red, white, and blue collars, dance round and round him. Steam rises from the cobblestones. The dogs are panting hard.

When people toss pennies into his hat, the man stops playing long enough to say, "God bless you, sir," or "A thousand thanks, good lady."

"We must hurry, Great-Aunt Elizabeth. No time to waste."

"Oh, Betsy," she pleads, "we *must* stop."

I grit my teeth and stop. The dancing dogs whirl around us. As they jump, they pant and gasp for air.

"The poor dears! I can see their ribs," my great-aunt cries. "My good man, you don't feed these dogs, and they're your bread and butter!"

"A penny, good lady," the man replies, "or a halfpenny will do, for an old man whose legs were shot to pieces while fighting next to General George Washington himself."

The man has been kicking up a little jig in accompaniment to his dogs. His legs look mighty sprightly for all their getting shot. He must realize what I'm thinking, for he stops dancing.

"Great-Aunt Elizabeth!" I shout in her ear. "We'll buy a bit of meat and bread for the dogs. After the quilt stall."

"The Misses Zane!" I hear Mr. Obadiah Bertram calling to us above the din. "The Misses Zane! Here I am!"

I pull Great-Aunt Elizabeth toward Mr. Bertram's quilt stall. He's waving to us and jumping up and down.

Jumping! In this heat! I push our way through the throng to his stall.

"Mr. Bertram," I say, "we're here at last."

"Miss Elizabeth Zane," he says, bowing to my great-aunt. "And young Miss Elizabeth Zane." He bows again.

Sweat is dripping down Mr. Bertram's nose. His shirt is soaked through and as translucent as candlewax.

"Surely there's a bit of air down by the docks, good sir," Great-Aunt Elizabeth gasps. "This heat is not Christian."

"One can only hope, Miss Zane," he replies in a booming voice, "hope and pray for an early autumn."

We shake out a quilt. Mr. Bertram clicks his tongue admiringly as he traces his finger along the quilting.

"Nineteen . . . twenty . . . twenty-one . . . twenty-two stitches an inch! There's not another needlewoman in Philadelphia with your skill, Miss Zane."

Great-Aunt Elizabeth beams at him. Then she raises her eyebrows. "And what of Betsy Ross Ashbourne, Mr. Bertram?"

Mr. Bertram laughs. "Mrs. Ashbourne is a seamstress, Miss Zane, not a quilter. Flags are one thing, Philadelphia winters are another."

"I remember when Betsy Ross Ashbourne could barely thread a needle," says my great-aunt. "Of course, that was before Mrs. Bingham and I started the Ladies' Quilting and Soldiers' Aid Society. We used to quilt for those wretched men in the War of Jenkins' Ear. Or was that the Seven Years' War? Why, I remember a young soldier with a terrible cough, whose coat was in tatters. Such a sweet face he had. . . ."

I sigh. How many times have I heard the story of the

young soldier with the terrible cough, who received Great-Great-Grandfather Karl Zane's Danish wool overcoat with the silver buttons as a present? Dozens of times, I reckon.

Mr. Bertram, who has surely heard this story as many times as I have, listens politely as I look away. The candle merchant in the next stall is packing up. His candles are actually melting in the heat.

" . . . and that was well *before* the Boston Tea Party. We had proper tea in those days, Mr. Bertram, as we quilted into the wee hours. We needed proper tea to stay awake. Why, one evening—"

"Great-Aunt Elizabeth, Mr. Bertram has other customers," I shout. "It's time to go home."

"No one wants to listen to an old woman's stories," my great-aunt says, giving me a hard stare. "Everyone's in such a hurry these days. It's the war, I suppose."

Mr. Bertram pays Great-Aunt Elizabeth a pretty penny for her quilts. It seems odd to be paid in British crowns, half-crowns, shillings, and pennies, but our American money is no good now. Our neighbor, Mr. Frye, says we don't have the gold to stand behind it.

We stop at the butcher's to buy a bit of beef for the dancing dogs. I find four stale rusks at the bakery and bargain the baker down to a halfpenny for all of them.

I follow the fife music to Front Street, pulling Great-Aunt Elizabeth behind me. I'm so hot, I feel as though I'm melting, just like those candles.

I toss the dogs the food. Despite their master's cheerful music, the dogs pounce on the meat and rusks at once, snarling and glaring at each other as they wolf down their dinners.

Their master stops playing his fife and looks at the last bit of beef. The growling dogs are having a tug of war with it. He licks his lips. Perchance we should have bought him food, too.

I help my great-aunt into our carriage. When I came to Philadelphia, she was as stalwart as a Virginia oak. Now Great-Aunt Elizabeth seems as light as the cotton wool with which she fills her quilts.

"We deserve a treat," she says gaily. "To Bradford's Coffee House, Maybelle. Trot on."

"It's too hot for coffee," I say crossly. "Can't we please just go home? Please? I promised Maybelle and the Merry May that I'd take them for a swim in the river. And don't ask her to trot. Maybelle's much too old to trot in this heat."

"A lady should never use such a peevish tone of voice, Betsy," she scolds. "You know I'm quite fond of coffee, now that there is no longer proper tea."

"There's no proper coffee, either." I try not to sigh too loudly. "All right. Maybelle, walk on."

Bradford's Coffee House is on Water Street, just facing Penn's Landing. I hitch Maybelle to the post, help Great-Aunt Elizabeth down from the carriage, and pull the heavy door open.

Bradford's Coffee House is cluttered with gazettes and pamphlets, cups and saucers, sailors and soldiers, sugar and sawdust. We each drink a small coffee, and we share a maiden's fruitcake. "Maiden's" means that no rum was used to preserve the fruit—the British won't allow the rum ships from Barbados to dock here anymore.

Bradford's coffee is really toasted cornhusks ground to a powder. It tastes like burnt corn mush. Since the embargo there's been no proper coffee, chocolate, or tea, no lemons, limes, or pineapples, no English china, no French silk or wine, no Spanish olives or capers, no Portuguese sherry, no pepper, cinnamon, cloves, or mace from the Spice Islands, no Flanders lace, no chintzes, calicoes, or palmapores (those hand-painted cloth borders for quilts) from India. Nothing but coarse homespun cloth, raspberry-leaf tea, burnt-corn coffee, and dry-as-toast fruitcake. How I wish this war would end.

I watch the men trying to cool themselves. They hog the coffee house's windows—splay-legged on the benches, backs pressed against the tables, shirts opened to the waist—fanning themselves with their tricorn hats. They gulp at their tankards like horses at a watering trough.

We Philadelphia ladies are obliged to sit with our knees together, our backs as straight as ramrods as we sip hot coffee. Great-Aunt Elizabeth tries to fan herself with a lacy trifle no bigger than a chicken's tail feathers.

I turn my face toward a mere baby's breath of a breeze blowing through the wharf-side windows. But Great-Aunt Elizabeth spoils the cool air by going on and on about proper tea.

"In the old days we had proper tea at every table, Betsy: breakfast, dinner, supper, and always a lovely spread for high tea. Proper tea, mind, none of that sassafras root or raspberry leaves! I've put away my mother's blue-and-white Swansea tea service. Do you remember the teapot and coffeepot, the cream pitcher, the sugar bowl, and all those pretty cups and saucers? After the war I'll take them out again.

"I was with her when she bought the entire set in Mrs. Lemon's china shop. Such a clever woman; she always gave her customers a lemon after a purchase. Every week we went back to buy something small, such as a toothpick holder? or a teaspoon? just to get that lemon. I remember . . . "

How awful to be old, I think grimly, to know the best part of your life is over.

Great-Aunt Elizabeth is still yammering about tea sets, wars, lemons, and hard times as I help her into the carriage and climb aboard the driver's side.

"Maybelle, walk on."

It's high noon, I reckon, and a herd of pigs has bunched under Maybelle, perchance hoping for shade. She gives them a listless kick. They squeal indignantly and trot away.

"Maybelle, walk on," I say again, giving the reins a shake. "Let's see the Merry May."

Her head down, Maybelle strains at the traces, then plods down Market Street toward Third and Church Streets. The heat shimmers back at us from the brick buildings on either side, turning the noonday into an oven. Sweat pours off my forehead and stings my eyes. It drips off my chin.

Maybelle's flanks are streaked and frothy with sweat.

"Oolong tea with lemon is the best, Betsy, with just a hint of sugar, and made with water that's not quite on the boil. . . . "

Aaron and Rab Morris gallop past us, Rab in the lead. It's against the law to gallop down the streets, but of course the young bloods race every chance they get. Their horses splatter garbage and dung onto my lap, hands, and face.

This is too much! My best summer muslin covered in muck! I throw the reins into Great-Aunt Elizabeth's lap. "Will you stop blithering about tea for a moment and drive?" I shout.

I use my handkerchief, in vain, to wipe my face, hands, and dress. My favorite lace handkerchief is as dirty as the rest of me.

"When will I go home?" I ask bitterly. Only then do I notice that we're not moving. My great-aunt is watching me. Even Maybelle has turned her face around for a better look.

"Never in my life have I been addressed so rudely," Great-Aunt Elizabeth says quietly. "For a lady to use such a tone of voice is unthinkable. What has gotten into you? You are as prickly and sulky as a mule."

Quietly and without a show of anger she takes a handkerchief out of her reticule and wipes her face and hands.

"I'm sorry, Great-Aunt Elizabeth. All morning I've thought about Virginia, my brothers, and my departed parents. I miss them all terribly," I reply.

My great-aunt doesn't say anything for a moment. "Of course you miss them, Betsy," she says. "But this is a heartlessly cruel world we live in, and it's a lady's purpose to make it less so. Do you understand?"

"Yes."

"No, you do not," she says kindly. "You are much too young yet, and for that you should be grateful."

She gives the reins a snap. "Maybelle, walk on."

We ride in silence. In our courtyard Great-Aunt Elizabeth hands me the reins and goes into the house. I back Maybelle into the carriage stall, unhitch her, and dump the traces, reins, and bridle into the tack box. The leathers will be a tangled mess tomorrow, but today I'm too hot to care.

As I lead Maybelle into her stall, her daughter, the Merry May, looks at me pleadingly from hers. She scrapes at the stall boards with her front right hoof.

"I know you're hot, May. I won't be a moment."

I run upstairs to my room, take off my dress, and use it to wipe the dung and mud off my arms and face. I kick off my shoes, roll off my stockings and ties, and change into my lightest summer dress. I leave everything on the floor for Old Bess to wash.

As I let Maybelle and the Merry May out of their stalls, they need neither my lead nor my encouragement. Mother and daughter trot onto Market Street, canter down the three blocks, and jump off the embankment. I run after them, panting.

In a few moments I see them, sunk to their withers in the Delaware River. If this were the Ohio and not the Delaware, I'd strip to next to nothing and go in after them. But there are too many people about. The sailors and soldiers on the wharf watch me, a look of hope on their grubby faces.

As I climb down the embankment, they give voice.

"I'll hold yer frock for ye, m'dear!"

"I'll hold anything else you'd care t'leave on shore!"

"I'll hold you, m'darlin'!"

The men shout louder as I wade up to my knees. The river smells as bad as the streets, but at least the water is cool.

My great-aunt will have a fit—two soiled dresses in one day. But I don't care if I soil a score of dresses. All I can think about is cool water.

I jump all the way in. The water on my hot scalp and neck feels delicious. My tortoiseshell hairpins float out of my curls and sink before my fingers can catch them. Great-Aunt Elizabeth will have another fit, for hairpins are impossible to replace these days. When I come up for air, I hear the men shouting their disappointment.

The horses and I swim for a long time. Maybelle finally scrabbles her way up the embankment. She shakes herself just as a dog would, then nibbles grass as she waits patiently for her daughter and me.

I begin to feel hungry. Oh, no! I was so hot this morning, I forgot to shop, I think in horror. We need everything—flour, potatoes, eggs, apples—we've nothing to eat at home.

I climb onto the Merry May's back. She snorts in surprise but settles down again once she finds her footing.

"Good girl, good May," I say softly. I use my knees to lead her toward the shore. "The wilderness, May! How I long to quit Philadelphia! If this were the Ohio, I could swim unfettered by hairpins and muslin dresses.

No one would care if I didn't behave as a Philadelphia lady all day.

"The air smells of pine sap, and there's more clover than you could ever eat. No Rab Morris and no pigs.

"I'll get us all out of Philadelphia, May, I promise. We'll gallop along the Ohio, faster than the wind."

2

Escape

After I put up Maybelle and the Merry May, I wring out my dress onto the stableyard's cobblestones. The muddy water hisses and steams. My footprints mist away as I walk toward the house.

The kitchen hearth fire is banked down to glowing coals, but the kitchen is still the hottest room in the house. Young Sam and Old Bess watch me come in.

"Young Sam," I announce, "my great-aunt and I didn't go shopping after all this morning. I was too hot to remember."

Young Sam looks up from knife cleaning in alarm. He knows what's coming.

"So you'll have to go in my stead. Just a few things for supper. Eggs and some flour for biscuits, that's all."

"They lookin' for soldiers, Miss Betsy, for fightin' in General Washington's army," says Young Sam.

"They won't enlist you."

"The Society been askin' for volunteers," he says under his breath. I can hear the eagerness in his voice. Great-Aunt Elizabeth does not know that Young Sam goes to the Rising Sun Tavern every chance he gets for meetings of the Pennsylvania Society for Promoting the Abolition of Slavery.

"We need you here, Young Sam, what with the war on and no Zane men in Philadelphia anymore. Here're some pennies. Quickly, now."

"Hotter'n Hades," he mutters, just loud enough for me to hear. The kitchen door slams shut.

Old Bess has been sitting at the kitchen table, shelling beans and listening to her son, Young Sam.

"A letter for you, Miss Betsy," Old Bess says.

"Mail?"

"In the parlor."

A battered, folded-up sheet of paper rests on the sideboard. "It's from Eb, it's from Eb!" I shout. I've been waiting fifteen months for this letter.

I run upstairs to my room, dripping water all the way. Great-Aunt Elizabeth's door is shut tight; she always takes a nap in the afternoon.

I throw myself on the bed and begin to read:

Zane Station
Fort Henry
The Ohio Company of the Commonwealth of Virginia
November 12, 1780

"November! How can a letter take nine months to deliver?" I mutter.

"'My dear sister,'" I read aloud.

We have just received your letter of May 22nd. I'm surprised there is any mail at all, what with the war.

I know how vexed you are staying with Great-Aunt Elizabeth, and I have thought hard about your request to quit her and return to Zane Station. Stay where you are, dear sister. I am not able to say more, lest this letter fall into enemy hands.

Please remember how much we love you and how much we care for your safety. Your brothers, your sister-in-law, your nieces and nephew, and I all wish you well.

Sad news. Despite all our precautions, Isaac has been taken captive by the Wyandot again. We should have sent Isaac with you to Philadelphia years ago. But he's a Zane and needs the wild country.

Your brother,
Ebenezer

I crumple the letter and throw it across the room. "I need the wild country, too!" I cry, punching my pillows.

"Betsy," my great-aunt calls from across the hall.

"I'm all right," I shout back angrily. "Go back to sleep."

"Betsy?"

"Coming," I shout. I am no better than a slave.

Great-Aunt Elizabeth is in bed with all her quilts piled up on top of her. With her hair down and her face powder wiped off, she looks ancient, and sick.

"You must be sweltering under those quilts," I say crossly. "Let me pull them off you."

"Leave them." Great-Aunt Elizabeth reaches out from the depths of the quilts and grasps my hand. Her fingers feel like icicles. She's panting for breath.

"That letter," she gasps, "addressed to 'Miss Elizabeth Zane.'"

She read my letter! She thought it was addressed to her!

She gives me a grin and tries to talk between pants. "You're just like . . . Nathaniel, your father. As wild as any Indian. . . . Just as Eb wrote . . . Zanes need the wild country."

"I'm—I'm sorry you read that letter," I stammer.

Great-Aunt Elizabeth shakes her head. "There's nothing for you here, child. . . . Just an old woman . . . two city horses . . . and two house slaves. Praying that I'll free them . . . when I die."

She looks at me sharply. "Manumission . . . is a scandalous business, Betsy," she says. "Freeing a slave is like freeing a cow—neither can take care of herself."

"Young Sam and Old Bess are here. Whatever do you mean, Auntie? You are not going to die," I say in a shaky voice. "I'll fetch you another quilt."

She won't let go of my hand. "I've tried to take care of you, Betsy. You would have made . . . your parents proud. A proper lady. You make . . . me proud."

"But Great-Aunt Elizabeth, *I've* tried to take care of *you*."

I hear a soft chuckle from deep within the quilts.

"Neither one has done . . . a good job, then. Folks aren't very good . . . at taking care of each other. Try we must . . . but we always fail. Help me . . . sit up."

I pull her up from the recesses of her feather bed. Her hands are icy cold. She's never struggled for breath like this.

"Great-Aunt Elizabeth, a doctor, I could—"

"Never forget, Betsy." She looks at me sharply. "Only you can take care of yourself . . . because only you know . . . what you really want from life."

She grips my hands harder. Her left eye looks peculiar, the pupil as wide as an open barn door. Her left hand looks peculiar, too, curled up like a hawk's claw.

"I'm so sorry about this morning, Auntie," I cry out, my voice breaking. "I was just feeling sorry for myself. I have never deserved your unblemished generosity."

"No, no," she whispers. "You're young . . . and you deserve your youth. Everyone does. . . . We have only the one chance. If you didn't yearn for adventure . . . you wouldn't be a Zane."

Great-Aunt Elizabeth sinks back into the feather bed and closes her eyes. She does not let go of my hands.

She whispers, "Talk to me . . . about . . . our good times."

"Our Danish Christmases," I blurt out, "amid all this Quaker austerity. Michaelmas. Ambles through Penn's Woods . . ."

"Christmas Day. *Juledag*," she says, smiling. "We gave those Quakers . . . a fair bit of gossip . . . for round the tea table, didn't we?"

I smile back at her. "That we did. Shall a fetch a doctor?"

"No cure for birthdays, child. . . . It won't be long."

"Surely I can fetch you something. Auntie?"

"If only we had some proper tea. I promised myself . . . that I'd have proper tea again . . . before I died."

Near the stroke of nine my great-aunt begins to gabble like a baby. Then the left side of her face collapses, as though a horse had kicked it in.

I send Young Sam to fetch a doctor.

When I hear his knock, I open the door and lead Dr. Benjamin Rush upstairs.

Dr. Rush looks at her face and lifts her left hand. When he lets go, it drops to her side. He motions me out of the room and closes the door softly.

"It won't be long," he says.

"That's what she said," I tell him anxiously. "It's really true, then, Dr. Rush?"

He studies my face. "Are you alone in the world, Miss Zane? Is there anyone else you can stay with?"

"My brothers."

Home! I'm going home! My heart beats quickly.

"Do they live in Philadelphia, Miss Zane? Shall I fetch them?"

"They live on the Ohio River."

"And you mean to join them?" Dr. Rush asks in alarm. "Among the savages and British marauders?"

"I was born in the Virginia wilderness. I'm going home."

"There is nothing I can do for your kinswoman." Dr. Rush shakes his head sadly. "Your great-aunt worked in the soldiers' hospitals in war after war. Miss Zane tended the wounded by day and quilted blankets far into the night. A remarkable woman: always a cheerful word and a kind hand. A lady. She's lived longer than most. Lovely quilts. My wife admires them so."

"Yes, a lady," I repeat softly. "Your wife may have her choice of the quilts."

"You are too kind, Miss Zane."

21

I escort Dr. Rush out onto the front steps. The town crier, Mr. Thomas Riggs, calls out, "A quarter to eleven, and all's well," just as I'm shutting the door.

Young Sam and Old Bess stand in the hall watching me. Old Bess is holding a platterful of biscuits with butter and jam.

"Supper!" I exclaim. "I forgot to eat."

In the dining room, slowly chewing on biscuits and drinking watery raspberry-leaf tea, I wait for my life to change.

I love Great-Aunt Elizabeth, but I can't help thinking that if she were to die soon, I could be at Zane Station before the first snow. Great-Aunt Elizabeth has lived all her days in Philadelphia. She was born in this house. She will (I reckon) die in this house. Unlike the rest of us, she's never needed the wilderness.

I couldn't live the rest of my life the way she has hers—I'd curl up and die. And yet she's been happy. Great-Aunt Elizabeth has taken good care of others, but she's also taken good care of herself. She's always known exactly what it is she wants.

If you didn't yearn for adventure, you wouldn't be a Zane.

I go upstairs, sit by her bedside, and read *Robinson Crusoe* to her. I read aloud far into the night. I sit at her bedside until her breathing stops.

I open a window to let her soul escape. The night air feels cool. Philadelphia at this hour is almost as quiet as the Virginia wilderness.

The town crier walks by. "A quarter to five, and all's well."

"Mr. Riggs," I call out, "my great-aunt has just died."

"I'm sorry for your loss, Miss Zane," he calls back. "I'll pass Dr. Franklin's offices in a few moments. Perchance he'll post your news in today's *Pennsylvania Gazette*."

"Thank you, Mr. Riggs."

I lie on my bed and go to sleep immediately. I'm too exhausted for tears, for plans, for dreams.

"Miss Zane. *Fraulein*."

Herr Dr. Casper Dietrich Weyberg, the pastor of the German Reformed Church, clears his throat. He is standing by the hearth. It's late morning, and the sunlight streams through the parlor windows. My eyes are dry and grainy from lack of sleep.

"The ancient Hebrews," Herr Dr. Weyberg says, examining his boot leather as though he'd never seen anything so fascinating, "were instructed by their priests to bury their dead before the next sunset. The heat in the Holy Land can be fearsome."

"Yes," I say in a hollow voice.

Old Bess comes into the room with a pot of raspberry-leaf tea and the rest of last night's biscuits.

My temples are throbbing. The hour is not yet eleven, but the heat is already as fierce as yesterday's.

Old Bess is watching me, waiting for instructions. I almost look behind my shoulder, half expecting Great-Aunt Elizabeth to be standing there giving orders.

"Pour Herr Dr. Weyberg and me a cup of tea," I say softly. I turn to him. "You were talking about heat?"

He clears his throat again. "A quick burial . . . has its practical side, *Fraulein* Zane. It's for the . . . the well-being of the community."

What on earth is he babbling about? I have so many things to do: the burial, renting the house, packing up.

The burial, and something about fearsome heat . . .

"You're talking about Great-Aunt Elizabeth," I exclaim. "She'll rot in this heat?"

Herr Dr. Weyberg says quickly, "The Burial Society will be here soon. I took the liberty of sending word, having read about your great-aunt in today's *Gazette.*"

The pastor heads toward the door. "I'll see you at six this evening at Franklin Square. Our cemetery is there. Your aunt bought her plot years ago. Under the biggest chestnut tree."

After he leaves, Young Sam joins his mother in the parlor. They stand as straight and solemn as sentinels.

"I am sorry for your loss, Miss Betsy," Old Bess says, with no expression in her voice.

I know what they want, of course. William Penn, who died in 1718, raised eyebrows by freeing his slaves, John and Jane, one month after his death. Since then manumission edicts have become the fashion in Philadelphia.

And just last year the Pennsylvania State Assembly passed the Abolition Act, emancipating anyone born to a free woman after 1780. This is 1781, and Old Bess was born fifty years ago, Young Sam sixteen years ago. They are both disqualified.

"Sit down, both of you."

For the first time ever, Young Sam and Old Bess sit in the parlor chairs they've spent a lifetime repairing and polishing.

I begin, "Great-Aunt Elizabeth asked that I not free either one of you. It was her dying wish. I'm to take care of you now."

Young Sam looks at his feet. Old Bess's eyes fill with tears.

I lean forward in my chair. "I mean to join my brothers in Virginia, now that Great-Aunt Elizabeth is gone. It will be difficult. We'll have to cross the Cumberland, then take a flatboat down the Ohio; wild animals, Indian partisans of the British army, the winter coming on."

Old Bess takes Young Sam's hand. "My husband is here," she says, her voice breaking.

"Yes, I know. Freeman David Porter is a fine man. Young Sam, you've been dreaming of joining the army, haven't you?"

He looks up at me in alarm but says nothing.

They don't want to come with me. All right, then.

"To be perfectly blunt, I don't want to take care of either one of you. I can only wonder how I'll care for myself, crossing the wilderness. So if you don't want to accompany me . . ."

They catch their breaths and look at me in wonderment.

"That is to say, why shouldn't Great-Aunt Elizabeth's death mean your freedom, too? I think I must free both of you."

Old Bess and Young Sam burst into tears. Their unfettered joy astonishes me. We Zanes have taken such good care of them! All I can do is sit and wait for them to stop. They just cry harder.

"As long as you'll be cared for," I say loudly above their sobbing. "That's Great-Great-Grandfather Karl's musket above the fireplace, Young Sam. You can have it."

Young Sam smiles and dries his eyes with his sleeves. "That's a blunderbuss, Miss Betsy. It's 'bout rusted solid. Nobody shoot one of them in a hundred years. But thank you, thank you!"

"If you're willing, your name is Mr. Samuel Zane and half of yesterday's quilt money is yours. When you're ready to leave, I will have the Freeman Letter for you. Guard that letter with your life, Mr. Zane. It will be the only proof of your freedom."

Samuel Zane runs into the kitchen. I hear the clatter of coins falling into his palm. I hear him counting out his share.

"Old Bess, your husband Old Sam is at Zane Station."

She dries her eyes, too. "Your parents sent for Old Sam sixteen year ago. He never even seen Young Sam. My life is here, with Mr. David Porter, my new husband."

"You'll stay with him, then? He'll take care of you?"

"Thank you, Miss Betsy, thank you!"

"If you're willing, your name is Mrs. Elizabeth Zane Porter, and you can have the other half of the quilt money. You'll need a Freeman Letter, too, should you wish to travel beyond Pennsylvania someday. I need paper and ink."

Mrs. Elizabeth Zane Porter stands up. "Paper in the drawer, ink in the jar."

I look up at her, surprised. Her gaze locks into mine,

and for the first time today, I feel like laughing. "Well, Mrs. Porter," I say with a grin, "it appears I'll have to get my own paper and ink from now on."

Our former slave stands tall and for the first time in our lives laughs with me. "I reckon that's true, Miss Zane."

The Burial Society comes this afternoon. They try to carry Great-Aunt Elizabeth's coffin up the staircase, but the casket is too wide. After a lot of head scratching and arguing in German, the biggest of the men carries Great-Aunt Elizabeth down to the parlor. I see the linen winding-cloth, flung over his broad shoulder like a meager sack of laundry.

I stay in the kitchen and cringe when I hear the soft thump as her body falls into the coffin.

Once they take their leave, the house is quiet. Too quiet. Young Sam and Old Bess have tied up their belongings in old quilts and left. I spend the rest of the day in the stable, bathing and grooming my horses.

It's just Herr Dr. Casper Dietrich Weyberg, the Burial Society, and me at graveside. Great-Aunt Elizabeth's friends are either long gone or too frail for a walk to the burial-lot on such a stifling evening.

Dr. Weyberg drones on. It's much too hot to pay close attention. Halfway through the service I notice Old Bess and Young Sam standing at the cemetery gate. I nod to them. They nod back.

Great-Aunt Elizabeth always hated having the same given name as her slave. I find myself thinking of the Mother Goose rhyme:

Elizabeth, Elspeth, Betsy, and Bess,
They all went together to seek a bird's nest;
They found a bird's nest with five eggs in,
They all took one, and left four in.

Elizabeth, Elspeth, Eliza, Liza, Liz, Lizzie, Libby, Liddy, Liv, Beth, Bessie, Bess, Betty, Betsy, Betts—there are plenty of ways to be Elizabeth in this world. And Old Bess was born in our house, just as Great-Aunt Elizabeth was.

What can they be thinking? I ask myself. Do they feel as free, and as lonesome, as I do?

Only then do the tears come. I cry for Great-Aunt Elizabeth, whose long life still wasn't long enough. I cry for Old Bess and Young Sam, whose lives are just beginning. I cry for myself, so alone.

After the funeral I walk down Fifth to Chestnut Street, to the Pennsylvania State Assembly, and hang my own Declaration of Independence, my own Freeman Letter, on the outside wall:

ATTENTION! GOOD GENTLEMEN!!
A young lady desires the safety of companions in order to join her family, before the first snow if possible, at Zane Station, near FORT HENRY on the OHIO

RIVER, of THE OHIO COMPANY of the
COMMONWEALTH of VIRGINIA. Will pay her
fare and passage for her chattel. To wit: two horses, a
carriage, and household effects.

> *Please inquire:*
> *Miss Elizabeth Zane*
> *Third and Church Streets*
> *August 23rd, 1781*

For the first time in my life I sleep in a house that is
absolutely empty of all souls save me.

3

Secrets

Name's Crofter."

A grim-faced man stands at the back door, hat in hand. Despite this morning's heat he's wearing a thick cloth wrapped high around his neck.

"Yes, Mr. Crofter? May I help you, sir?" I ask.

"Here to help *you*. This yours?"

He holds up my notice. The weather has been rainy these last few days, and it is a smeary mess of mottled ink and soggy paper.

"Yes, sir. That's mine. What's left of it."

"Aim to build a toll road," Mr. Crofter says. "The Crofter Road, from Philadelphia to Pittsburgh, for pioneers headin' west after the war. You goin'?"

"Are—are you offering to accompany me to Pittsburgh, Mr. Crofter?" I stammer.

He looks at me blankly.

"Goin' or not?" He shakes the paper for emphasis; inky water sprays onto the hem of my dress. "I need ta know."

"I need to think." I wish he hadn't taken my notice down. "Please, come in."

Mr. Crofter steps through the kitchen and into the dining room. He takes a hard look at the mahogany table, chairs, sideboard, and highboy. He gazes up at the polished brass-and-crystal chandelier.

"Two more stories got ye?"

"Yes, sir."

He shakes his head. "Six rooms full o' dainties won't fit onto two horses."

"I'll not take the furniture, the silver, nor the china, Mr. Crofter. The Virginia wilderness is no place for dainties, as you call them."

"Dainties," Mr. Crofter says, looking at me from head to toe. "Ya been?"

I look him straight in the eye. "I was born in the Virginia wilderness, Mr. Crofter. It is Philadelphia that seems strange."

"Wild and brawny, are ye?"

"Yes, I suppose so," I say, smiling at him. "But Mr. Crofter, will anyone else be accompanying you from Philadelphia to Pittsburgh?"

"Nay."

"Then I couldn't possibly—"

"None but m'wife and our six bairns."

"Oh. Your family?"

"Aye."

I study him as he studies me. The hall clock strikes eleven times to mark the hour.

"All right. I'll go with you, Mr. Crofter. A halfpenny a mile to Pittsburgh," I say briskly. "The horses will forage along the way."

Mr. Crofter opens the door. "We leave tomorrow. First thing."

"Tomorrow sunrise? I have an entire household to dispose of! There isn't time."

"Sunrise." The door slams shut.

The church—the church and Herr Dr. Weyberg! I slap a black mourning shawl around my shoulders and run out onto Market Street. I turn down Fourth and run past the Mikveh Israel Synagogue to the German Reformed Church.

On the way home, I call on Sarah Peabody to say good-bye.

"Betsy, please don't leave me! Please!"

"Sarah, you've always known I'd go home someday."

Sarah is weeping into her apron. "Don't forget me."

I put my arms around her. "I haven't time to go and bid our friends good-bye. Would you tell them I'm leaving at tomorrow's dawn? Abigail, Jane, Belinda—they can stop at Zane House. I'll be home all day."

I whisper into her ear, "I'll never forget you."

Sarah's crying so hard, I wonder if she's heard me.

But all day long friends pay calls to say farewell. I give four of Great-Aunt Elizabeth's best quilts to Abigail Levy and ask her to give them to Mrs. Benjamin Rush.

The Zanes have lived in this house for one hundred years. Karl Zane left Denmark under a cloud, but he took plenty of worldly goods with him to sweeten the pain of coming to Penn's Woods.

I've often wondered what I would take with me when I

finally went home to Virginia: Clothes? Keepsakes? The most useful? The most costly? The most portable?

I lay out seven quilts in the parlor and run higgledy-piggledy upstairs and down all afternoon. On the quilts I pile dresses, chemises, underdrawers, bonnets, stomachers, soap, winter wraps, Great-Great-Grandfather Karl's blunderbuss, his helmet and chest armor, shoes and stockings, brushes and combs.

I gather up the quilt corners and bind them with ropes. They look like the dumplings those Lancaster Amish eat by the bowlful with chicken and noodles.

Chicken and noodles! I'm starving! With Old Bess gone I've had to make do with briar jam spooned from the jar, wine jelly, and raspberry-leaf tea.

I loosen the ropes and cram a sealed-up blackberry-jam jar into the center of each quilt. The wine jellies are free-standing, with just a cloth over each to keep out the dust. I stand in the larder and eat them one by one. I feel floaty and muzzy headed.

The silver trays from Denmark! I reckon I could carry one under each arm.

The bijouterie, jewels, and bibelots! I run upstairs, burst into Great-Aunt Elizabeth's room, and dig into her jewelry box with both hands. The Baltic-amber earbobs, the pearl necklaces, the gold bracelets, the tiny alabaster elephant (the symbol of the Danish Crown), the gold and mother-of-pearl snuffboxes—I have to have them all. I run downstairs with the jewelry box and cram it into another quilt.

Great-Great-Grandfather Karl's letters from William

Penn! The letters have been in the upstairs desk since Philadelphia's charter. The hundred-year-old paper crumbles like pie crust as I stuff the sheaves into a quilt bundle.

Great-Great-Grandfather Karl's portrait! I pull it down from the parlor wall. We Zanes all look alike, with black hair and eyes so dark as to be almost black. I can't leave the portrait behind.

I cut the canvas out of the frame with a kitchen knife, roll it tight, and stuff it into a quilt.

The bridles, reins, and saddles! I run into the stable, cursing the setting sun. Maybelle and the Merry May shake their heads and whinny. "My darlings, there's no time for a swim today, I'm sorry," I call out as I drape tack around my neck and stack saddles on my left arm.

Belinda Weymouth stops by and puts the kettle on for tea. I sit in the parlor with her to drink it. I'm hot, thirsty, and tired, but my mind is like a runaway horse. I just can't rein it in. While Belinda talks about our school and her mare's chestnut foal, I'm thinking of dozens of things I have to do before sunrise.

The seven quilt bundles are now as big as Cotswold hogs. Belinda helps me loop the bridles and reins around the quilt bundles, but there is no place for the saddles. I'll have to carry them (on the silver trays?) or find a way to stack them onto my horses' backs.

This morning I offered Herr Dr. Weyberg our Philadelphia house as a hospital. Anything I don't take with me is his—or rather, is the property of the German Reformed Church.

"What am I going to do?" I ask Jane Raffles, who has come to say good-bye. "Maybelle and the Merry May will never consent to hauling seven bundles through the forests and over the mountains." I wave my arm. "And all the rest of this, too?"

"I could keep it—" Jane begins.

"A letter!" I shout.

I find a sheet of paper and begin to write:

To Herr Dr. Casper Dietrich Weyberg,

In my haste to join my family, and in my grief over our loss, I now realize that I spoke rashly about our household effects.

After the war my traveling companion, Mr. Crofter, intends to build a toll road from Philadelphia to Pittsburgh. Perchance when that road is finished, and the war is over, you could send our household chattel to Pittsburgh via that road, then flatboat it down the Ohio?

Many thanks,
your parishioner,
Miss Betsy Zane
Zane Station (Fort Henry)
Virginia

"There," I mutter to myself. "Surely there will be a proper road through the wilderness someday."

I look up, half surprised to see Jane sitting across from me.

"You've already left us, Betsy," she says, her eyes shining. "Go to your wilderness. We all knew this day would come." She gives me a hug, then looks around the parlor. "We've had so much fun in this very room: our Shakespearean theatricals, our tea parties. I'll see myself out, Betsy. Good-bye. And good luck."

After graining and watering Maybelle and the Merry May, I spend the rest of the night winnowing seven quilt bundles into four. Karl Zane's armor, helmet, and blunderbuss sit on a parlor chair, looking like a hundred-year-old ghost.

Before sunrise, I grain and water the horses again. They look surprised to be fed so early.

"Eat up, my darlings," I tell them. "It's a long way till your next meal. You'll be eating leaves and thistles for weeks to come."

Our carriage! Our beautiful carriage will gather dust for years! Herr Dr. Weyberg will, I hope, never use anything so fancy to carry wounded soldiers. I split some empty grain bags with a kitchen knife and cover the carriage the best I can.

At sunrise Mr. Crofter appears. He helps me lash my four bundles to the horses, two bundles each. I've got saddles draped across my arms. We walk down Chestnut Street to the Pennsylvania State Assembly, where his family is waiting. I'm sweating, and my shoulders and arms already hurt.

Sitting next to the driver's box, Mrs. Crofter nods to me sleepily. The six children are huddled, still sleeping, I reckon, in a spacious Conestoga wagon drawn by four draft horses. There are a few bundles in the wagon, nothing more.

"Mr. Crofter, you didn't tell me you had a near-empty wagon," I say angrily.

"Ye didn't ask."

"You gave me the impression we were walking! I brought only what I could carry!"

Saddles tumble to the ground.

"No room for dainties," Mr. Crofter answers, climbing onto the driver's box. He takes the reins in his hands.

"Mr. Crofter, a moment, please." I close my hand around the lead horse's bridle.

"Pittsburgh won't wait, Miss Zane."

"Pittsburgh *will* wait!" I snap at him. A few Crofter children sit up and turn their heads toward me. "I promised you: no furniture, no silver, no china. But I've left sweet feed in our stable. The mice will have eaten it by Christmas—wouldn't you rather the horses have it?"

Mr. Crofter scowls. His wife and the six children, now wide-awake and fanned out behind her, look at me curiously.

"We'll go back for the grain. Wallace," he says shortly. The oldest Crofter boy flings my saddles into the wagon.

We return to the house I thought I'd never see again. The parlor and kitchen windows seem to be looking at me in surprise. I enter the front door and scoop up a pile of silver spoons and knives from the parlor floor.

No silver.

This silver will have to be my secret, I tell myself with a smile, dropping the spoons and knives into my dress pockets. My letter to Herr Dr. Weyberg is still propped on the shini-

37

est, fanciest silver tray. Already the house looks empty and abandoned, with forsaken treasures scattered on every surface.

Money! I run to the kitchen and scoop coins from the secret compartment under the sink. I rush upstairs and look for one of Great-Aunt Elizabeth's reticules. The one for evening, a pretty bag of black lace and satin, is under the bed. I drop the coins in, pull the drawstring, knot it, and loop the ribbon around my neck.

Mr. Crofter and his eldest son are loading the grain into the wagon. Quickly, I untie the quilt bundles from Maybelle and the Merry May and hoist them into the wagon, too.

Mr. Crofter climbs into the driver's box again and glares at me. "Pittsburgh won't wait," he says flatly. He jerks his thumb back toward the wagon.

"I prefer to walk . . . for a while, Mr. Crofter."

"Suit yourself."

The wagon is in motion before I remember to tie my horses to the backboard. I can't lock the house, because I forgot to give the spare house key to Herr Dr. Weyberg.

"Surely he'll come around this morning," I say to myself. "Surely everything the Zanes own will be in safe-keeping with the Germans by sunset."

We pass the Pennsylvania State Assembly again on our way out of Philadelphia.

"There's no turning back now," I say.

The Crofters look at me warily and say nothing.

I remember someone else saying those very words in this very place. It was July 1776. I had just turned eight and had been living with Great-Aunt Elizabeth since April.

All that spring the delegates to the Continental Congress argued about our separation from Great Britain. Shall we have a king? Everyone else has one. Shall we all speak the same language by decree, and if so, which one, English or German? Shall the Quakers and Amish enjoy the same rights as their countrymen, as they are unwilling to fight for those rights?

On July second, Mr. Thomas Jefferson's draft of the Declaration of Independence was put to a vote. They voted, and voted again. July fifth passed, as did the sixth.

My great-aunt's quilting circle shook their heads over the delay. "Is this the best those macaronies can do?" Great-Aunt Elizabeth had snorted. "We ladies could have written the whole thing by May thirty-first, and thrown a stack of quilts into the bargain!"

Finally, on July eighth, the July fourth version of Mr. Thomas Jefferson's Declaration was signed by all but a few delegates. The Liberty Bell rang out thirteen times, in honor of the thirteen new states. As the people gathered round, Captain John Nixon read the proclamation.

We hold these truths to be self-evident, . . .

I remember Great-Aunt Elizabeth nudging me, saying, "Something to tell your grandchildren, Betsy."

. . . life, liberty, and the pursuit of happiness. . . .

But all I could think about was how homesick I felt, and how hungry I was. Old Bess's good cooking waited for us in the dining room. Feasting on her fried chicken, warm bread, briar jam, and butter, but at home in Virginia, was my idea of the pursuit of happiness.

One by one, the delegates walked out onto the cobble-stones to listen to John Nixon. They looked exhausted yet proud. As the last words died away, there were some cheers, but most folks just gaped back at them.

"There's no turning back now," someone murmured behind us. We walked home silently, the Liberty Bell ringing again in our ears.

———————

It's midday, I reckon, when we stop at the edge of a forest for our nooning. Except for Mr. Crofter, no Crofter has said a word to me all morning. They watch me with wary eyes.

Mrs. Crofter climbs out of the wagon. While the Crofter boys gather wood for a cook fire, I dig into a quilt bundle for some briar jam, then untie Maybelle and the Merry May. Mother and daughter, hock deep in lush grass and clover, crop and chew, crop and chew. The sweet smell of torn fodder fills the air.

The Crofter horses whinny, toss their heads, and strain at the traces; they want to graze, too.

"Shall I unhitch your horses, Mr. Crofter?" I ask. "Surely they've earned a good graze."

"Pittsburgh won't wait."

"The sweet feed will last longer," I reply, "if they graze."

Mr. Crofter stops stuffing tobacco into his pipe. He studies my horses for a while, then shrugs his shoulders.

I unhitch the Crofter horses. They bury their noses in the clover, too. I hobble the lead horse.

Our bacon, cornbread, and fried cabbage are ready.

"My name is Elizabeth Zane," I say in my best ladylike voice. I pass around a jar of Old Bess's blackberry jam. "But everyone has always called me Betsy."

Surely they'll introduce themselves now.

They don't.

It's been so long since I've had any real food that I gulp down everything on my plate with scarcely a chew.

"Who will be havin' more?" Mrs. Crofter asks.

"I will!" I say eagerly.

Mr. Crofter scowls at me. "Ye eat a lot for a lass."

"Since my great-aunt died Monday last, I've had nothing to eat but briar jam and wine jellies, Mr. Crofter."

Mrs. Crofter looks up from her frying pan. "Canna you cook nor bake, lass?"

I laugh. "Me, cook? I don't know the first thing."

"Didna your great-aunt teach ye how?" Mrs. Crofter nods toward her only daughter. "My Mary's been cookin' since she were five."

"Great-Aunt Elizabeth used to say a lady needn't know with what color her kitchen walls are painted."

The Crofter boys are looking at me in surprise. "However did y'eat, then?" the oldest asks.

"Our house slave, Old Bess, prepared all the food."

The entire Crofter family sucks air through their teeth with a loud hissing sound.

"Slavers, are ye? The Devil's own!" Mr. Crofter shouts.

"What nonsense! Old Bess and Young Sam are like family."

"So where are they now?" Mr. Crofter demands.

"Well, I freed them after Great-Aunt Elizabeth died. And . . . they . . . left." My voice runs down like a clock.

All eight Crofters nod their heads.

"Like family but not, that's why they left, first chance," Mr. Crofter says. "A terrible price this new nation of yourn will pay for slavin', you'll see."

"What nonsense," I say again, but with less conviction in my voice. I take a big gulp of water from my tankard.

"God won't sit for it, on His throne," the youngest Crofter pipes up. He looks to be about four years old and has a face as sweet as an angel's. His bright-blue eyes seem to look right through me.

"Not for long, God won't," Mrs. Crofter says firmly.

"You're eating Old Bess's briar jam," I announce.

The Crofters gasp at their pewter plates in horror. They turn their heads—their hair the color of marmalade—as one to look at Mr. Crofter.

Mr. Crofter puffs on his pipe thoughtfully. "God made the blackberries," he finally says. "And the blackberries didna know 'twas slave hands turned them t'jam. They still be God's good berries, only a bit . . . muddled-like."

"You'll be havin' more jam, then, Pa?" the oldest boy asks. I remember from this morning, his name is Wallace.

"Aye," Mr. Crofter grunts.

"Then so will I," says Wallace as he reaches for the jam jar.

It's just as steamy hot here in the countryside as it was in Philadelphia, but at least the heat smells better. I smell the sweetish scent of rotting wood and leaf mold. A breeze wafts by, carrying the fragrance of wildflowers and balsam.

The sharp smell of clean water makes everyone's nostrils quiver, horse and human alike. We stop at a stream for a drink before leading the horses to water.

Miss Crofter looks to be ten, maybe eleven. She climbs onto the back of the lead horse and clucks her into the deepest part of the current. The other horses follow, including Maybelle and the Merry May. They drink so much, and so quickly, that the water level drops for a moment.

"Mary, is it?" I call out to her from the stream bank.

"'Tis not your fault, Miss Zane," she returns. "Your family bein' slavers and all. 'Twas not your idea, surely, you being but a young lass. God forgives ye."

"Please call me Betsy," I say, delighted to be talking with a girl again. "Why are your parents so dead set against slavery? The English imported slaves to Pennsylvania. Are not the Crofters English?" I catch my breath. "You're not Tories, are you?"

"Betsy! We're Scots!"

"So . . . it's the Scots who are against slavery?"

"Some are." Mary studies me for a moment, as if deciding whether to tell me something.

"You have a secret, Mary," I say, grinning at her. "I can always tell. I'll tell you my secret if you tell me yours."

"Aye." Mary doesn't smile back. She jumps off the lead horse and pulls the mare to shore.

Mary pokes her face so close to mine, I can see the

bright flecks of blue in her irises. Her eyelashes and eye-brows are as white as snowflakes.

She whispers, "Back in Scotland, we were slaves."

My mouth drops open.

"Oh, aye. Didna you see the scar around Pa's neck? He's worn the iron collar since he turned thirteen. Pa couldna bear to have any son of his wear the iron collar. So before Wallace and Robert could come of age, Pa chose the thickest, rainiest day last January, and we ran. Been running ever since."

"That—that can't be true!" I exclaim.

"Oh, aye. Bound to the laird's coal mines for generations. Lord Balburn it was. We couldna leave. Pa paid an Irish sailor on board ship to cut the iron collar off with a handsaw. Cut him bad, it did."

"Indentured servants have to work for seven years without pay," I say slowly. "Don't you mean your family's indentured?"

"We're runaway slaves, Betsy. That's our secret."

"But you're as white as I." I clamp my hand over my mouth.

Mary looks at me steadily. "Aye."

"I'm sorry. Too often I speak without thinking first."

The horses drink. Water chatters over the streambed stones. Insects sing. Somewhere a frog croaks. The smaller Crofter boys giggle and splash one another. Unladylike remarks flit through my mind, each certain to be more cruel to Mary than the last.

"Your accent," I finally say, "the way you say 'laird,' it sounds a bit like 'lard.' Old Bess uses lard to make biscuits."

Mary throws back her head and laughs. "To tell ye the truth, Betsy, Lord Balburn had more than enough lard between his ears."

I grin at her. "The lord of lard?"

Mary faces east—faces Scotland, I reckon—and spits. "That's for the lord of lard."

4

Buffalo Roads

The rocking of the wagon lulls me to sleep. When I awaken, we are moving through deep woods. Great-Aunt Elizabeth's Tree-of-Life quilt has been pulled over Mary and me. One of my linen petticoats drapes our faces. Zane treasures are stacked neatly at my feet.

Mrs. Crofter is sitting next to us. "Awake are ye, Miss Zane?"

"I was so sleepy, Mrs. Crofter. I spent all night packing. Thank you for covering me. The black flies and mosquitoes would have eaten me alive."

"Lovely needlework on this quilt. Old Bess made these quilts as well?"

"No, Great-Aunt Elizabeth was the quilt maker."

Runaway slaves. No wonder the Crofters are so tight-lipped. And as thick as thieves.

Mary sits up and yawns.

"Mary says you're from Scotland." Under the quilt, Mary pinches me hard.

"Aye. Mister found work on the docks. Lived on Zane Street, we did."

I feel myself turning red, remembering the one-room

shacks and utter squalor of Zane Street. Worse still, did the Crofters ever see Great-Aunt Elizabeth and me in our fine clothes and fancy carriage, driving past on market Mondays? My bored, scowling face must have looked more haughty and disdainful than a queen's.

"Not a pretty street, but surely it used to be. A hundred years ago Zane Street was one of the first streets in Philadelphia."

"Was it, now?"

I'm glad to change the topic of conversation. "Will you stay in Pittsburgh or take a flatboat down the Ohio, Mrs. Crofter? I'll need passage to Zane Station."

"That's for Mister to decide. But Betsy, I don't know about those heathen savages out there in the wilderness."

"Most are heathen, but that does not mean they're savages! When they were children, my brothers were held captive by those same Indians. The Delaware and Wyandot taught them to be hunters and trackers. Jonathan liked living as an Indian: a new adventure every day."

Mrs. Crofter gasps in horror.

"After a few years of captivity, they were taken to Fort Detroit and ransomed back to my parents," I say quickly, not wishing to alarm her. "All except for Isaac. The Wyandot won't let him go because Princess Myeerah wants him."

Mrs. Crofter gasps again.

"But my brothers are fifteen to twenty years older than I, Mrs. Crofter. And times have changed; captives are rare these days. There's no finer place on the Ohio than Zane Station. Pure air, plenty of land for farming . . . um, fresh starts."

Mary pinches me again.

Mrs. Crofter says, "Aye, to fresh starts, then."

We stop for supper, and the Crofter boys scramble out of the wagon to look for firewood. While Mrs. Crofter and Mary prepare our meal, Mr. Crofter unhitches his horses, unties mine, and leads all six to a nearby glade.

The Crofter horses are cobs. I can tell by their dappled white coats, their deep withers, their full haunches, their calm natures. They've got hooves the size of pie plates.

Mr. Crofter loves them dearly, that's plain. He talks to them softly as he strokes their flanks. He tears clover out of the ground and feeds it to them by hand.

"Fine team, sir," I say. "A family, I'd guess."

Mr. Crofter's face softens as he watches them. "Aye, they be that, Miss Zane. The lead is their dam, Lady. And that be Laddie kickin' up his heels. 'Tis his sister Lassie rollin' in the clover. The youngest is Lobbet, still close to her mother."

"Mary says you're from Scotland. Scots cobs, are they?"

"Scotland?" He frowns at me. "Nay. American cobs they be."

I'm itching to ask him how a runaway slave could possibly have the money for such a handsome team of horses. But Mr. Crofter is as forbidding as a judge—I dare not ask him. Maybe Mary will spill their tale, if she's tipped in the right direction.

All the next day and the next I walk alongside Mary,

asking more and more questions about their lives in Scotland. We walk far behind the wagon.

"Were *you* a coal miner?" I ask.

"I stayed home and took care of the wee ones."

"And your mother?"

"Aye, she worked the black seam."

"Your mother was a slave?" I whisper.

She turns to me. "Betsy," she says softly, "miner or no, we all were slaves. When we were baptized, my parents bound us to the laird forever and ever. My brothers would have worked the mines. I would have worked the pit, too, when I was older."

"If your father spent his life in a coal mine, how did he learn to read? He read my notice. Slaves can't read."

"The secret schools. On Sundays."

"Secret schools?"

"Aye." Mary tosses her head. "Surely a family of slavers would have been the last to know about the secret schools, Betsy."

"There aren't any secret schools in America," I announce.

"Sure of that, are you?"

I stop in my tracks. "No, I'm not sure," I reply slowly, thinking about Young Sam and his abolitionist meetings.

I have to trot a bit to catch up with her. "Mary, how did your father learn to drive horses?"

"After fifteen years in the pit, he was taught to drive the coal wagons. Twenty-horse teams, they were."

"How could he ever afford those cobs?"

"They're not stolen, if that's what you mean," Mary

snaps. Her mother, in the wagon, turns round to look at us.

"I didn't mean that. But how—"

"No more questions." Mary runs ahead of me.

"Mary, wait." I run alongside and gently take her arm.

"Please," I say softly. "I didn't mean to hurt your feelings. I gave a bit of money to Young Sam and Old Bess, along with their Freeman Letters. Young Sam joined the army. Old Bess has a freeman husband. They'll be taken care of. Who takes care of you?"

"Who takes care of *you*, Miss Betsy Zane?" Mary snaps.

"I take care of myself!"

Mary's eyes blaze cold fire. "Oh, aye. The mistress of your fate. And we Crofters can't do the same, then?" She wrenches her arm away and runs toward the wagon.

Stunned, I stand alone on the Crofter Road. Far ahead, Mr. and Mrs. Crofter sit tall in the wagon, their heads craning forward. All the better to see their very own road, and their future, too, I reckon, spreading out before them.

Surely, Young Sam, rifle in hand, is drilling in the army by now. Old Bess is sharing the bounty of her own table with her own husband and in her own home.

Great-Aunt Elizabeth was wrong, I think suddenly. Slaves aren't like cows. They *can* take care of themselves. They dream their dreams, plan their plans, just as the rest of us do. The difference is, they have to plan and dream in secret.

I run toward Mary again and take her hand. "Your father worked hard in order to buy the cobs," I say softly. "He must be very proud, tearing a road out of the very wilderness."

She squeezes my hand. "You'll be telling me *your* secret, Betsy."

"The Zanes claimed land in Virginia we call Zane Station, near Fort Henry, six days south of Pittsburgh, on the Ohio River."

"'Tis a threadbare secret you're telling me."

"My secret is this: No one knows I'm coming. My brothers could be away fighting in the war, for all I know. I have one sister-in-law, my brother Eb's wife, whom I've always called Aunt Bessie. Eb could have sent Aunt Bessie and their children back to New Hampshire."

"Your parents?"

"They were killed by the Indians," I whisper. "Don't tell your mother."

Mary grips my hand harder.

"I'll stay in the Virginia Zane House by myself if I have to," I say carelessly. And yet my heart quickens a bit. Could I really stay there alone?

"But the Indians, Betsy!"

I grin at her. "I won't tell them if you won't."

We've been wending our way to Pittsburgh for two weeks now, and I can't help but notice that there is a road of sorts already. We're on a trail flanked by massive trees, the size of kilns or smokehouses: Big enough to drive a team and wagon through if someone chopped a tunnel first.

There are smaller saplings on the trail. When we can't go around one, Mr. Crofter and his sons swarm over it like

51

beavers, gleefully felling it to the forest floor, chopping it into logs, then stacking them in the back of the wagon. As the wood dries a bit, we use it for cook fires.

This morning we awake to clear, dry air with a bit of a cold snap to it. My nose and lungs feel cool breathing it in.

Mid-September. I'll be home before the first snow!

"Mr. Crofter," I say at breakfast, "I've wanted to drive the cobs since Philadelphia. Would you let me try? I've been watching you carefully, and we must be close to Pittsburgh. That means time is running out. I've driven Maybelle since I was nine. Four horses can't be much harder than one."

"Wouldn't they now, Miss Zane?" There's a bit of a twinkle in his eyes, or maybe it's the reflection of the dancing firelight.

After breakfast I wait for Mr. Crofter in the driver's box. I plead and plead with him for miles.

Finally he gives me the reins. The cobs perk up their ears immediately; they know someone else is driving them.

Well. Driving Maybelle is much easier than a four-in-hand. Lady and Laddie list to the right as Lassie and Lobbet, the rear horses, slow down. Four pairs of ears peel backward toward me, listening for commands.

"Walk on," I command them. "Walk on, Lady. I mean, walk on . . . all of you. Please?"

"Nay, Miss Zane," Mr. Crofter says patiently. "Don't think o' them as four horses. Think o' them as two columns with two horses in each, the reins keeping them straight. They'll stay in pairs. You control Lady's pace, and her bairns will follow."

"I understand. Yes, that is better, Mr. Crofter."

I drive the horses for miles without speaking. As I gain the cobs' trust, they relax again. I must have gained Mr. Crofter's trust as well, for he no longer leans forward, ready to spring out of the driver's box. He reaches for his pipe.

"I think I have the lay of it now, Mr. Crofter," I say proudly.

"Aye, that you do. You're a good driver, Miss Zane."

"Thank you," I say, warming to his praise. "You told me you intend to build a toll road from Philadelphia to Pittsburgh. But isn't there a road here already?"

Mr. Crofter actually laughs. "Buffalo roads. These buffalo of yours have done most of my work already. You've discovered my secret, Miss Zane."

His secret! If only he knew!

He nods to the west. "Buffalo headin' west for the grasslands, or comin' home for the shade o' these brawny trees. Thousands of 'em been traveling back and forth for who knows how long? Since the Flood, I reckon. Animals always travel in a straight line to save their strength. Their road becomes mine."

I smile at him. "How do you know about the buffalo?"

"The laird's son used to talk about America all the day." He catches his breath. "I heard about the beasts," he says shortly. "Dinna remember when."

"You're a very good driver, too, Mr. Crofter," I say in a soothing tone. "But then, Mary said you used to drive a twenty-horse team, when you were bound—"

Oh, no! I clamp my hand over my mouth.

Mr. Crofter snatches the reins from my hands. The cobs stop in their tracks.

"Get out o' my wagon," he says coldly. "Mary! Come here!"

"We were just two girls trading secrets, Mr. Crofter. Don't blame Mary. Please, sir!" I cry. "Too often I blurt out the first words that come into my head. I'm sorry."

"GET DOWN!"

I jump to the ground. "Mr. Crofter, please!"

His face is chalk white in fury. Mary is trembling as she climbs in beside her father. Mr. Crofter cuffs her so hard, she falls out and onto her face.

"Mary, I'm sorry," I say as I help her to her feet.

"Leave me alone!" she shouts, wrenching her arm away.

I've lent Mary my best summer dress. The snowy muslin skirt and white lace stomacher are smeared with grass stains and mud.

Mary bursts into tears.

"Come here, lass." Mrs. Crofter hoists her daughter up beside her. I hold my arms up. Instead of helping me into the wagon, Mrs. Crofter looks away.

"Walk on!" Mr. Crofter shouts. The frightened cobs prance a bit, then bolt forward.

I bring up the rear of our party. I step carefully, of course, on account of the six horses ahead of me.

I will never, *never* speak without thinking again. All the rest of this day no Crofter will meet my eyes. I try to talk to them at our nooning, at tea, at supper. They turn away silently.

As I lie awake tonight under the wagon, it occurs to me that the Crofters might be afraid I'll turn them over to the slave catchers. I used to see runaway-slave bulletins posted on public buildings all the time. There's good money to be made, turning in runaways. And it's a flogging crime, to be a captured slave.

I could never turn them in—how could they think otherwise?

Something else hangs heavily among the Crofters besides fear. If it were only that, they'd be watching me, trying to figure out what I'll do. But no Crofter has looked at me all day.

Shame.

They're ashamed of themselves, having been found out as slaves.

In Philadelphia I could always tell if a man or woman was free. Freemen walk tall, with their heads held high. They look at you straight in the eye. They speak their minds.

But the Crofters have no Freeman Letters. They're not free.

They were counting on blending in, and you've spoiled their fresh start, Betsy. You've made a lonely girl betray her family's shameful secret by offering friendship instead.

That's why they're here, on the Crofter Road. If they're caught, at least they're all caught together.

Are Young Sam and Old Bess walking tall with their

heads held high? They never used to. That morning I gave them their Freeman Letters they wept for joy. And I thought I was freeing them for *my* benefit, not theirs. I was winnowing them out of my quilt bundles, in a manner of speaking.

"I had no idea," I whisper to myself, "no idea what a gift my life has been."

I roll over and sleep fitfully, feeling as lonesome as that first night after Great-Aunt Elizabeth died.

The next morning, as we're all sitting round the fire eating breakfast, I speak up.

"Mr. Crofter, we have a contract," I say in a shaky voice, "a halfpenny a mile to Pittsburgh."

He grunts.

"We Zanes don't know why our Great-Great-Grandfather Karl left Denmark to come to Philadelphia. We do know that he was the third son of a nobleman and that King Christian V had a hanging-warrant for his arrest. He never saw his home or family in Denmark again."

"You're a lady, then?" Mary interrupts, her eyes full of wonder, "the Lady Elizabeth?"

"I reckon. My point is, America's a hard land. Nobody comes here without good reason. Either to escape poverty or the law, whether that poverty or law be unjust or not. Folks come here for a fresh start. Surely that's what this war is all about?"

My face burns as hot as the cook fire.

"Mr. Crofter, we were Danes; I have no allegiance to the British Crown. I will never reveal your secret."

No one says anything. They all watch Mr. Crofter as he slowly cleans his plate of cornbread, Old Bess's briar jam, and bacon.

"Miss Zane," he finally says, "You're a steadfast, patient driver. And you've earned the cobs' trust; you may drive them again, anytime you wish."

"Thank you, sir."

For weeks now, the hot afternoons have melded together, and now the evenings are hot again, too.

Mr. Crofter and I take turns driving the cobs. We make frequent stops for water and food, both for our party and for the horses. Maybelle and the Merry May no longer try to pull away as I tie them to the wagon's backboard every morning. Our journey has become an arduous yet pleasant routine.

One steamy afternoon the younger Crofter children lie sleeping in the wagon bed. Wallace is walking next to the wagon, asking me questions about the wilderness and the Indians.

I'm driving the cobs, but I can scarely answer him, I'm so drowsy. Mr. Crofter snores beside me in the driver's box, his hat turned low and his chin on his chest. It's as still as the grave.

"Miss Zane, you're sayin' the Indians will cross the Ohio to attack the settlements, even though they sold that land to the Crown? Doesn't seem fair to me."

"It wasn't they who sold the land to the Crown. The

Iroquois sold it as part of the Fort Stanwix Treaty, back in 1768. The Ohio Indians say the Iroquois never owned the Ohio Valley to begin with. It wasn't theirs to sell."

Wallace whistles. "It sounds like their fight is with the Iroquois, then."

"Most of the Ohio tribes are allied with the Iroquois now, and fighting for the British."

Wallace shoots me a perplexed look.

"I know, it's all very confusing," I say.

We've been climbing a long incline all day. The horses are droopy headed and sweaty. The crest of the hill is just ahead.

"Do you hear that thunder?" I ask him. "It'll be raining and cool soon, and we'll be going downhill. The worst of today is over."

"I've never heard thunder like that."

"It does sound peculiar."

Very peculiar. Instead of stopping and starting, the thunder rolls and rolls, louder and louder.

The cobs mill about. Even slow-as-molasses Maybelle begins to prance and fret. The Merry May screams and throws her front hooves in the air. As Lady tries to walk backward, the rest of the cobs rear up in their traces. Mr. Crofter lurches to his feet and listens. The thunder is now a roar. "By St. Andrew," he shouts, jumping to the ground, "'tis the buffalo!"

"Buffalo?" I shout back.

"Down from the wagon, everyone! Run for the trees!"

We all jump down. Mrs. Crofter gathers up little hands and drags her screaming children deep into the woods.

Mr. Crofter and Wallace dash to the lead horses. Yanking at their reins, they pull Lady and Laddie to the left and well into the forest. The wagon is just off the road.

From behind a tree I can smell the buffalo. The rank stink of animal panic fills the air. Above the pounding hooves I hear the Merry May screaming in terror.

The cobs and the wagon are safe in the trees, but my horses are still on the buffalo road!

"A knife! A knife! My horses!" I scream, running toward the wagon. Maybelle and the Merry May are pulling at their leads, trying to break free. Our Irish-linen lead shanks are as strong as iron; mother and daughter will tear the back off the wagon first.

"Help me! Mr. Crofter, help!"

The buffalo have crested the hill: dark shapes in a cloud of dust.

Mr. Crofter is beside me, knife in hand. He cuts Maybelle's lead shank and off she goes, down the hill and away from the charging buffalo.

The Merry May rears up, tearing the top plank off the backboard, and gallops after her mother, the plank bouncing and splintering behind her.

The buffalo roar by. Two hundred, maybe more. They don't even look at us. Clots of dirt fly in all directions.

And then they're gone.

"Load up," Mr. Crofter shouts in the sudden silence. "Ellen, are the bairns a' right?"

"We can't leave," I cry out. "My horses will come back, I know they will."

"Miss Zane," Mr. Crofter says firmly, "the old girl was likely trampled to death. As for the young 'un, trailin' a plank like that, who's to say?"

"Maybelle can outrun any buffalo, and the Merry May has known me since the day she was born. I know they'll come back!"

"Pittsburgh won't wait."

I sink to my knees, sobbing with my arms outstretched. "Please, Mr. Crofter, please! I'm begging you! My horses!"

"Load up!"

"Mister," Mrs. Crofter says, coming out of the forest, "there's a fair creek in the woods back there. The wee ones are dusty, tired, and frightened. Surely we can stay here tonight."

"Ellen, be ye daft? It canna be three in the afternoon."

"Where's the harm in it?" Mrs. Crofter asks.

"They'll come back here and wonder why I've abandoned them!" I scream. "The wolves! The panthers! Mr. Crofter, please!"

"One night, Miss Zane. We leave first thing in the morning, with your horses or no."

I run down the long hill, calling to Maybelle and the Merry May. Buffalo hooves have bitten hard into the sod. Again and again I trip and stumble over the churned-up earth.

It's almost dark when I turn around, hours later, sick at heart. All I've seen are split-hoof buffalo prints. There are no rounded-hoof horse prints. There are places where the buffalo road opens into glades. Perchance Maybelle and the

Merry May left the Crofter Road at the first opportunity. All I can do is hope.

I rejoin the Crofters for another cornbread-and-bacon supper. I try to stay awake, but I'm weary from the day's trials and afflictions. I fall fast asleep.

When I awake at sunrise, Maybelle and the Merry May are cropping grass, as placidly as cows, along with the cobs.

"You came back. I knew you'd come back!" I stroke their noses as they nicker softly to me. I untie what's left of the plank the Merry May dragged along behind her and fling it into the woods.

I click to them and wrap my arms around a thick tree trunk. Maybelle and the Merry May take turns rubbing their itchy foreheads against my back.

"Do you see, I was right, Mr. Crofter!" I shout triumphantly. "I knew they'd come back to me. Thank you so much for waiting."

Under the wagon Mr. Crofter sits up and blinks at us, his mouth hanging open.

He shuts his mouth with a snap, then opens it to growl, "We load up after breakfast. Pittsburgh won't wait."

5

The Ohio

We reach Pittsburgh on Michaelmas, September twenty-ninth. Great-Aunt Elizabeth and I used to celebrate Michaelmas in the Danish way, with a feast. We'd start with a seafood stew made with herring, crabs, clams, and potatoes, sweetened with cream and seasoned with dill and caraway seeds. Old Bess would roast a goose stuffed with apples and red cabbage, which we call *rødkal.* Dessert would be *kringle:* butter pastries stuffed with custard, almond paste, and raisins, and dipped in vanilla icing. We'd drink beer and coffee if we had any.

Our Quaker neighbors used to stand in hands-on-their-hips disapproval right in front of our house. With frowns on their faces but their noses high in the air, they'd sniff at the cooking scents wafting out our windows. The Quakers think most holidays are from the pagan, or even worse, from Rome. But my Quaker girlfriends would always ask a thousand questions after each Michaelmas, St. Lucia's Day, Christmas, New Year's Day, Lady's Day, Easter, Pentecost, and May Day.

There is no feasting or revelry in Pittsburgh, sad to say. I doubt anyone here even knows it's a holiday. They're all too busy. The sounds of sawing and hammering fill my ears.

In haste the pioneers tear apart their wagons to build flatboats, sometimes called broadhorns. Every wharf, every dock, every berth is crowded with the hulls of flatboats in every stage of construction. A great mound of discarded wagon wheels lies just north of town.

A flatboat looks like a farmstead on a raft—walls and a roof, hearths and chimneys, even chicken coops and animal sties. Flatboats are bigger than wagons, so pioneers are obliged to buy more lumber to finish them. Stacks of lumber for sale lie along the water's edge, piled as high as houses.

Pittsburgh is where the Allegheny and Monongahela Rivers join to form the Ohio. With the strength of three rivers, the mighty Ohio pulls the pioneers' flatboats downstream.

When Eb brought me to Pittsburgh when I was seven, Three Rivers Island was so thick with trees, it looked heavy enough to sink. Now the island is as bare of trees as Penn's Landing back in Philadelphia. On the highest cliff, like an eagle keeping its eye on a teeming nest of mice, sits Fort Pitt. The garrison used to be British, but now it's American—it's ours.

Riverside, everyone and his brother has something to buy or sell, sometimes both. I hear cries of "Solid oak pegs, and the finest Pass and Stow nails sold here!" and "An expert carpenter here! Will trade work for bed and board."

A scout in greasy buckskins and a bearskin hat pulled low on his brow shouts, "The best riverman on the Ohio, at your service. I've navigated to Fort Randolph and back a dozen times."

There are draft horses on offer and pigs for winter hams. Yards are full of chickens and sundry fowl for sale. Thanks to the army supply routes, the trading posts look ready to burst with muskets, shot, and gunpowder, tobacco, kettles, pots and pans, tubs of lard, bowls, spoons, knives, candle molds, saws, hammers, washtubs, bolts of cloth, needles, and thread.

The pioneers buy and buy. Mrs. Crofter buys needles and thread, a bolt of broadcloth, some flour and lard.

One woman has half her cabin filled with rosebushes for sale. I buy a middling-size bush for Aunt Bessie. My choice has a few dried, reddish petals still clinging to the rose hips. The roots and soil are tied up neatly in coarsely woven linen.

"Soak the roots once a month or so this winter, and come spring plant it in a sunny spot, that's all," the woman says. "Roses only look delicate. The truth of it is, they're as hale and hearty as weeds. Grind up those rose hips once you've reunited with your family. Make a rose-hip tea, and you won't take sick all winter."

I nod politely, but I can't imagine drinking what's been pruned off and thrown away after the flowers have died.

"Don't pull a face, young lady," the rose woman says. She slips my coins into her none-too-clean stocking and wags her finger at me. "You just remember what I said when you're laid up with the ague come January."

Back at the wagon, Mrs. Crofter admires my rosebush. "What a beauty, Miss Zane. Plant her in a pride of place."

"I will, Mrs. Crofter," I reply eagerly. "The south side of the Virginia Zane House has full sun all day. We'll have roses from May to October."

We've been in Pittsburgh for only a day and a half, and already Mr. Crofter is restless. He runs his hands along the spokes of the wagon wheels to test for weaknesses. He cranes his neck toward the eastern hills—to scout for bad weather, I reckon. Phantom reins dance in his hands.

"Mr. Crofter, are you sure you won't buy a flatboat and come with me to Zane Station? It's the best place on the Ohio."

"I'm sure it is, Miss Zane. But the Crofter Road needs a lot more work if I'm to take on paying customers less accommodating than you. We'd best be gettin' back before the first snow."

I smile at him. "Philadelphia won't wait?"

Mr. Crofter looks eastward again and smiles. "Aye, Philadelphia won't wait. We Crofters've come a long way, Miss Zane. Once the feet get used to walking, 'tis hard telling them to stop."

"I understand."

After our supper Mr. Crofter and I go down to the riverside to find the broadhorn that will take me home. He tells me he'll study the men on board for pluck, river skills, and sobriety. I want to see the livestock stalls.

On board the broadhorns I open grain bags to be sure they contain oats, corn, alfalfa, and molasses. Feed merchants have been know to slip sawdust into their sweet feed. I have none left, since giving the rest of mine to the cobs.

Mr. Crofter makes sure the hull planks are hammered fast with wooden pegs, not iron nails. Wooden pegs will expand and contract in consort with the planks. Nails won't.

We return to the wagon, Mr. Crofter shaking his head. "Not a decent riverman among them, Miss Zane. They know no more about riverin' than I do."

"I saw a scout who claims to be a riverman. He says he's been to Fort Randolph and back a dozen times. He certainly *looked* woodsy enough. I could hire him."

Mr. Crofter whistles. "And he'd float ye in yer own flat, like Queen Cleopatra of old?"

I smile. "No, I'll find another party to travel with."

"Aye, Miss Zane, but it'd mean askin' a man to give up his rudder, an' you know how men are," Mrs. Crofter says softly.

"I'm hearin' you, Ellen," Mr. Crofter shouts.

"I'll ask the scout's advice about rudders," I say.

I find the scout on the riverbank, watching the Ohio side. Long and thin, with an aura of menace about his person, he reminds me of the musket barrel he's leaning on. His hair is a wonder—a long, black braid trailing almost to his knees.

"Are you the river scout, sir?" I ask politely. This autumn has been sunny and warm, but just as he turns toward me, a cloud blocks the sun.

"A poke in the eye!" he shouts. "I'd know that pretty face anywhere. It's Betsy Zane!"

I step backward in shock. "I—I don't know you, sir."

"Not surprised," the man said grimly. "I must look a bit rustic. I've been laying low in the woods since April." Here his voice drops to a whisper, "On account of killin' those two Delaware chiefs, Betsy. Both armies want to hang me, and the folks downriver are riled up too, can you believe it?"

I just stare at him.

"Aw, Betsy." The scout has tears in his eyes. "You really don't remember me? We grew up together." He leans toward me and whispers, "Lewis Wetzel."

Lewis Wetzel! The last time I saw Lewis, I was a child, and he was pulling the legs off a spider, just to see how many it could lose and still try to run away from him. I'd like to run away from him, too, but I need a river scout.

"Lewis! Of course I remember. I didn't recognize you with such a . . . a rustic look about your person."

A hunted look is more like it. His eyes, lighter than his skin and wide in panic, shift from side to side. He hunches his shoulders and gives his bearskin hat another tug, the better to hide his face. His lower lip is bloody from gnawing on it.

His bloody lip reminds me of the time Mr. Wetzel decided it was high time to turn his boys into mountain men. He took Lewis, Jacob, and Martin far downstream and left them there on shore. Six days later the brothers were standing before their father's threshold, chewing on great chunks of raw, bloody wolf. Lewis couldn't have been more than nine, his brothers eleven and twelve.

When I explain my situation, Lewis leaps into the air, so eager he is to help.

"Don't you fret. We'll find the best broadhorn in Pittsburgh. You'll be with your brothers within a week. I promise you, Betsy."

"I've been traveling with a Scots family, all the way from Philadelphia. Mrs. Crofter says no man will give up his rudder."

Lewis Wetzel laughs. "You leave the rudder to me."

"Look whom I've found. A friend of the family," I say. We are back at the wagon. The Crofter boys are staring hard at Lewis. Mr. and Mrs. Crofter are reeling back in horror.

"This is Mr. Lewis Wetzel. I've known him since I could walk. Lewis, this is Mr. and Mrs. Crofter and their children."

Lewis gives Mr. Crofter a salute. "Captain? Ma'am? We Virginians are much obliged to you for bringing Betsy back to her rightful home. Zane Station hasn't been the same since she left."

Mr. Crofter eyes Lewis's buckskins, dried stiff with sweat, bloodstains, and grime. A fearsome assortment of knives and hatchets hangs in clusters from his belt.

"We best be goin', Betsy," Lewis says, glancing at two soldiers as they walk by.

"I thank you, Mr. Crofter." I hold out my hand, full of shillings and crowns, to him. He slips the coins into a pocket.

"Good-bye, Mrs. Crofter. Good-bye, Tommy, Robert, Douglas, John, Wallace. It was a pleasure traveling with you on the Crofter Road. Good luck. Watch for those buffalo."

I take Mary's hand. "I know you'll take good care of yourself, Mary."

She gives my hand a solid squeeze. "That I will, Betsy."

"Wallace will help you tote your things," Mrs. Crofter says. "Good-bye, Miss Zane." She eyes Lewis again. "Good luck."

"I'll be fine, Mrs. Crofter. Really, I will. He's a friend of the family."

Mr. Crofter clears his throat and ducks his head. "Miss Zane, straightaway it was 'Mr. Crofter,' and 'sir,' with ye. I thank ye for that. No lady has called me 'sir' in m'life."

———

Lewis Wetzel jumps on board a finished flatboat and walks over to the rudderman, hand outstretched.

"Captain? I was born on the Ohio. Miss Zane wants a scout to take her to Zane Station and Fort Henry. You goin' that far?"

"Beyond it," the man says, folding his arms in front of him. "I've a brother-in-law at Fish Creek Flats."

"I know Fish Creek Flats." Lewis calmly scratches his

beard. "Captain? See those hills over there on the Ohio side? More Indians in those hills than ticks on a dog. We can't see them, but they's watchin' us. Shawnee, most likely."

The man stares at the Ohio shore.

"The thing is—where'd you say you were from?" Lewis asks him.

"Elizabeth, New Jersey."

"Pretty name, one of my favorites. But I reckon there're no Shawnee in Elizabeth, New Jersey?"

"I can't say there are."

"Seems to me," Lewis says slowly, "you've got a choice. I can hold the rudder and keep us out of arrow shot. I know these currents and sandbars well enough. Or I could do the shootin'. Trouble with shootin' is, it's after the fact."

Lewis looks meaningfully at the man's wife and children.

"That is," he says, "they'd be shootin' at us already."

The man juts out his chin. "I'll have the rudder. It's my flatboat." His wife tugs at his coat sleeve.

Lewis shakes his head sadly. "Captain? I was held captive by those same Shawnee as a lad."

He pulls his buckskin shirt down to reveal a long, white scar along his collarbone. "I got this scar from a knife fight with none other than Tecumseh himself. We were just boys back then. Every day I thank my Maker I'm still alive. You don't want to hear my stories, Captain, especially in front of these tender children. So which one will it be? Shootin' or rudderin'?"

The man looks at Lewis's scar, me, my horses, and my quilt bundles. His gaze rests again on Lewis's scar.

70

"A halfpenny a mile," I announce.

Lewis says, "That's eighty-eight miles, Captain, free and clear. The Zanes have the money."

"We're the Westbys," the man says finally. "You can do the ruddering. What did you say your name was, sir?"

"I didn't."

At sunset we tie up on the Pennsylvania shore.

After supper Lewis Wetzel and I sit by the fire. The logs rest on a slab of firestone so the fire can't burn through the deck. The Westbys are snoozing in hammocks. In the stalls, Maybelle, the Merry May, and the Westbys' horse are stretched out in fresh straw, sound asleep. Their pigs and cows wheeze and snore.

Lewis tells me about the last seven months, how he's been hiding out from settlers and the military, both British and American, and living as a solitary in the wilderness.

"I snare rabbits because I can't risk having my gunshot heard. Last summer I was jabbering to the blue jays and grasshoppers, Betsy. Just to make sure I hadn't lost the knack for speech."

"Why did you kill those Delaware, Lewis?"

Lewis Wetzel is sitting against a post, in darkest shadow. I can't see his face. "They were Indians, Betsy."

I shiver despite the fire's heat. "Lewis, the Delaware took such good care of my brothers! What were their names?" I ask.

"Killbuck and White Eyes."

I have read of these men. In the *Pennsylvania Gazette*, Dr. Franklin praised them as Delaware elders—sachems—respected and listened to on all sides. The Ohio tribes have sided with the British, who have promised them the land itself if Britain wins this war. But if we win, we'll need all the Indian friends we can get. No wonder both armies and the settlers are angry with Lewis.

"I thought those Christian Delaware were neutrals," I remark. "Killbuck and White Eyes were fighting for the British, then?"

"No one's ever neutral, Betsy. You remember that."

After a short silence I say, "I must have been about five or six when you were taken captive. Do you know what my brother Eb said about it?"

"I don't believe so."

"He said, 'Eleven-year-old Lewis Wetzel has been taken captive by the Shawnee. May God help the Shawnee.'"

I hear a low chuckle from the shadows.

"What will you do, Lewis?" I ask. "Do your parents still have their farm on Wheeling Creek?"

"Never been much for farming. And I'd hate to put the old folks in danger."

It would be impolite to tell him that his troubles are his own fault. According to Eb's none-too-frequent letters, Lewis has hated Indians ever since he and his brothers were taken captive by the Shawnee. All he wants is revenge, and any Indian will do.

"I'm sorry, Lewis. Good night."

"Sweet dreams, Betsy. You're a sight for sore eyes."

You're not. The sooner I'm away from you, the better.

The next morning, our broadhorn hugs the Pennsylvania shore, edging close to the sandbars. I'd forgotten about the stands of immense trees. Mighty windstorms have ripped some of them right out of the shoreline. They lie half hidden in the river, their gnarled roots dangling higher than our heads.

And the Ohio shore? Remote and mysterious, it might as well be the Japans. Fog hangs in layers on the slopes and shrouds the hills in leaden silence.

Lewis Wetzel is an excellent rudderman. We never wedge up against sandbars. We never curve into the rapids.

I spend the time grooming my horses. I talk to the Westby children about the wilderness. They ask question after question about the animals and the Indians.

On the fourth day Lewis tosses his cap in the air. "We're almost there, Betsy," he yells. He does three hand-springs, lets out a couple of war whoops, grasps the rudder again, and begins to sing:

Come all you pretty maids, spin us some yarn,
To make us some nice clothing to keep ourselves warm.
For you can knit and sew, my loves, while we do reap and mow,
When we settle on the banks of the lovely Ohio.
There's fishes in the river, just fitted for our use.
There's lofty sugar cane that will give to us its juice.

There's every kind of game, m'lads, also the buck and doe,
When we settle on the banks of the lovely Ohio.

"Teach us that song," the youngest Westby boy shouts eagerly. "Sing it again, sir!"

"There's plenty more verses," Lewis returns.

All ye girls of New England, who are unmarried yet,
Come along with us and rewarded you shall get.
Through the wild woods we'll wander and hunt the buffalo,
When we settle on the banks of the lovely Ohio.

I can't imagine Lewis settled anywhere.

On the fifth day settlers wave from their cabin window. I see their smokehouse, clothes drying on sticks, a rude horse paddock, pumpkins and squash shining in the fields. Another cabin comes into view as the Ohio wends its way around a sandbar.

"Settlements," Lewis grumbles. He lets go of the rudder. "Captain Westby? Ma'am? Betsy? Good luck."

Holding his musket and powder horn in the air, Lewis jumps off the back of the flatboat and onto a tangle of downed trees. A few steps onto the riverbank and he's gone, vanished into the underbrush.

Mr. Westby lurches for the rudder just as the broadhorn begins to slip sideways into the current.

"Thank the Lord we're rid of that one," Mr. Westby says. "He's as cozy with the Devil as I've ever seen on this earth."

"His name is Lewis Wetzel," I reply grimly. "Tell your brother-in-law Lewis Wetzel was your rudderman. He'll have something to talk about all winter."

On the sixth day I see Wheeling Island in the middle of the river. A few moments later Fort Henry and the Virginia Zane House appear high on the cliff.

I shout, "The Zanes! The Zanes! It's Betsy! Ebenezer! Andrew! Jonathan! Silas! Isaac! Aunt Bessie! I've come home."

6

The Zanes

Mr. Westby steers the flatboat to the leeward side of Wheeling Island. He turns the broadhorn sideways and slows us down as we reach the dock. I jump out and tie us fast.

My brothers spill out of our house and charge down the hill toward the riverbank. Watching them run, I try to figure out who's who. In their buckskins and raccoon caps, their knives and pistols slung through their belts, they look so much alike—tall and thin, dark haired, dark eyed, with that strong Zane chin that bespeaks resolve (or stubbornness, some say). They haven't changed at all.

Jonathan unloads my horses. Silas sets my quilt bundles on the dock. The saddles lie like overturned turtles in the sunshine.

"Where's Andrew?" I ask. "Have you news of Isaac?"

Using her oar, Mrs. Westby pushes off into the current.

"Stay near the Virginia shore, the Westbys," I shout. I toss Great-Aunt Elizabeth's reticule, with the last of my money, on board the broadhorn. "Thank you and good-bye."

"Fare thee well, Miss Zane," Mr. Westby shouts, his

voice floating behind him. Already he's casting a weather eye on the Ohio shore.

"Where's Andrew?" I ask again. "Where's Isaac?"

"Andrew is on the Ohio side, scouting for the army," Silas replies. "Isaac is still a captive of the Wyandot. Betsy, what are you doing here?"

"Great-Aunt Elizabeth died in August," I say, trying to keep my face suitably mournful but brimming with happiness. "I'm home! I've come home at last."

Ebenezer gives one of my quilt bundles a little kick. "And what of our household effects, sister? Our Philadelphia chattel?"

"There's no way to tote furniture overland, Eb."

"So where are they?"

"I gave our chattel to Herr Dr. Casper Dietrich Weyberg. We used to attend services at his church—the German Reformed Church on Fourth and Race Streets."

"You gave away everything we own to those Germans?"

"For now, Eb. For safekeeping, I mean."

"Safekeeping!" Eb shouts. "With Germans? How many times have they marched into Denmark, declaring her their own?"

"You've rented out the Philadelphia Zane House?" Silas asks.

"Not exactly. Our pastor needs a soldiers' hospital, for the war. He'll give it back."

"YOU GAVE AWAY OUR HOUSE?" Jonathan roars.

"What were you expecting?" I shrill back. "The feather beds? The silver tea service? The mahogany highboys, chairs, tables, and sideboards? The Swansea china? I've come all this way," I say, my eyes filling with tears. "All I've wanted for years and years is to come home, and all you can think about is what I've left behind!"

Eb narrows his eyes at me. "Where is Great-Great-Grandfather Karl's blunderbuss? His helmet and armor?"

"Young Sam said nobody shoots blunderbusses anymore—"

"The *Germans?*" Jonathan groans. He throws his raccoon cap on the dock and stomps on it.

Eb looks downriver at the Westbys' flatboat.

"Betsy," he says softly, "where are Young Sam and Old Bess?"

"They're free, of course," I reply, in a voice much braver than I feel. "Everyone is freeing their slaves these days."

My brothers stare at me. Out of the corner of my eye I see Aunt Bessie coming down the hill toward the dock, a clutch of children behind her. Old Sam and his Virginia wife, Rachel Johnson, follow the children.

"Young Sam wanted to join General Washington's army," I say. "Old Bess has a new husband now, a Philadelphian named David Porter. He's a freeman, and blacksmith, a good one. He used to shoe Maybelle and the Merry May in trade for Old Bess's cooking and her company."

"You gave away all our property!" Eb shouts. "The furniture, the china, the slaves. Our carriage! WHERE IS OUR CARRIAGE?"

I squirm uncomfortably. "I covered it with feed bags,

although Herr Dr. Weyberg will need a way to tote wounded soldiers to the hospital."

"To Weyberg's hospital? To our house in Philadelphia, you mean," Eb roars.

"Betsy," Silas cuts in, "we need Young Sam and Old Bess. The work out here is endless."

"They were proud to have their freedom," I reply. "Young Sam felt honored, having a chance to fight for his country. Old Bess loves her new husband. And besides, the Pennsylvania State Assembly abolished slavery just last year. It's the law now."

"Abolished slavery for whom?" Eb demands.

"Pennsylvanians." I decide to say nothing about Old Bess and Young Sam not being qualified.

"That settles it! We're Virginians!" Eb shouts. "Old Bess and Young Sam are the property of Virginia gentlemen!"

"Young Sam and Old Bess are Philadelphians," I say with a throb in my voice. I can feel the tears returning. "They've lived there all their lives."

Eb bellows back, "They're not Philadelphians, they're property!"

"We're as poor as church mice," Silas whispers in horror.

Eb, Silas, and Jonathan stand in front of me like three wolves who've cornered a rabbit.

"Aren't you even glad to see me?" I wail at them. "I've wanted to see you for ages. I faced dour Scots and charging buffalo . . . and—and Lewis Wetzel. I almost lost my horses. Because all I've ever wanted is to come home."

My brothers turn their heads as one and look upstream, as though expecting another flatboat laden with Zane treasure and slaves to round Wheeling Island. I begin to cry.

Aunt Bessie nudges them aside and holds out her hand to me. She still has her wheat-colored hair, her warm brown eyes.

"Aunt Bessie, surely you're glad to see me, even if my brothers are not," I sob.

"Betsy, of course I'm glad to see you. How you've grown, and into such a beautiful young woman."

She glares at my brothers. "Virginia gentlemen do not shout at their long-lost sister. Betsy has come home at last, and all you can do is torment her. You should be ashamed of yourselves."

Aunt Bessie folds me into her arms. Her children stare up at me, wide-eyed.

"Welcome home, Betsy," she whispers in my ear. "Possessions don't matter. People do."

7

Myeerah

The frost nips the pumpkins, the early-morning fog dances on the river, and I'm rested to distraction.

Eb insisted that I needed at least two weeks of bed rest after my ordeal. It was useless to argue with him.

"My removal from Philadelphia was not an ordeal," I tried to explain my first evening home. "It was an adventure. I'm not the least bit tired."

"Young ladies are delicate creatures, sister. You'll not go out until you've lost that wild look to your face."

"You've not rested two weeks in your life!"

"I'm not a frail young lady," Eb replied.

"Neither am I," I said through clenched teeth. "Jonathan and Silas, can't you talk some sense into him?"

They regarded each other.

"Some folks are hard of hearing," Silas began.

"But Eb's hard of listening. Don't you remember that, Betsy?" Jonathan ended.

"I'm not seven years old anymore, Eb. I should know if I'm needing rest or not. Eb?"

Ebenezer leaned back in his chair and shouted toward the kitchen. "Rachel! Any more of that squirrel stew?"

So . . . I have spent these eleven days pacing in the same bedroom I had as a girl, way, way up on the third floor. I share this bedroom with my nieces: seven-year-old Elizabeth and five-year-old Sarah. They and my nephew, four-year-old Noah, visit me on occasion. Silas and Jonathan have come up, too, raccoon caps in hand, to apologize for their dockside behavior.

Fort Henry is just sixty yards away from my eastern window. Soldiers drill every morning; I watch them hoist our colors up the flagpole. They fetch water, shine their boots and buttons, march in formation, and practice at war by bayonetting haystacks.

I can see the blockhouse, where the ammunition is stored, about forty yards from the main gate of Fort Henry.

I remember my father planting apple trees. His orchard is now as tall as the second story of Zane House. The golden October air is scented with apples.

I have been practicing my delicate-young-lady face in front of the mirror. The frailer I look to Eb, I reckon, the faster I'll be free. I let my mouth go slack to smooth my jaw. I pat Aunt Bessie's rice powder on my cheeks to pale my face. My eyelids droop to half-mast to give my countenance a spiritless look.

All the while I'm muttering to myself, "I've got to find a way around Eb. I've got to see the Merry May."

I look outside my window and stamp my foot. The forests are ablaze in late-October color. Maples, buckeyes, chestnuts, and poplars are golden yellow. The oaks are brilliant red, the ash trees are the color of plum cake. Autumn frosts have killed the deer flies, horseflies, and black flies. The winter storms have not yet turned the ground to slick mud. The crisp air sets a horse's legs to dancing. October is the best time for riding.

The Merry May knows it, too. I hear her kicking the stall walls and whinnying for me.

I stamp my foot again. I didn't come all this way just to be locked up like a princess in a fairy tale! I had more freedom on the Crofter Road. Even Great-Aunt Elizabeth let me come and go as I pleased.

The only way I'll ride today, the only way I'll get around Eb, is if I look like I've got one foot in the grave.

Rachel Johnson cooks, serves all the meals, and helps take care of the children. I sit down at the table just as she is serving up the ham and biscuits.

Her eyes widen in surprise.

This morning I have rubbed a deathly pallor of layer upon layer of rice powder on my face. At table I pretend to be a dying princess. As pale as whey, I do everything slowly: eating, talking, drinking my sassafras tea. I let my head sort of droop, like a flower in want of watering.

"Look at this," Eb says, shoving a piece of paper under my nose. He has taken no notice of my sickly countenance.

I read aloud:

Mr. Weyberg,
I understand my empty-headed sister gave away our house, and all our household effects, including two slaves, to your church. Please under-

stand that she had no right to give away property that did not belong to her and that J, Ebenezer Zane, declaring rightful ownership of said property, have given away nothing.

We Zanes will pay for the transfer of all our property, including the two slaves, to Zane Station, Virginia. You may include this list as an invoice and bill-of-lading.

Sincerely,
Ebenezer Zane
Zane Station
The Ohio Company of the Commonwealth of Virginia
October 22, 1781

Below the date Eb has made a long list of household effects, with Young Sam and Old Bess at the very top. Great-Great-Grandfather Karl's blunderbuss, helmet, and armor, snuffboxes, porcelain commodes, tea chests, teacups, coffee grinders, coffee cups, creamers, salt cellars, candle snuffers, cutlery, stewpots, the silver trays, feather beds, pillows, good china, everyday china, highboys, tables, chairs, the carriage . . . the list goes on and on.

I am *not* empty-headed, I feel like shouting, but I catch myself in time. *A dying princess—sickly, pale, and wan.*

"Quite an accounting," I say softly.

"While you've been resting, I've been after Old Sam to remember everything from the Philadelphia Zane House. He remembers most of it. Including his wife," Eb says dryly. "That should light a fire under your Herr Dr. Casper Dietrich Weyberg."

"I did not give our chattel to the pastor," I reply, trying

to keep the anger out of my voice. "I did not give Young Sam and Old Bess to anyone, save themselves."

"We'll see about that. Now," Eb says, tucking the letter under his plate, "what in tarnation's wrong with you? You look like death warmed over."

I look up, startled. "May is ready for some air," I say softly, looking at my plate again. "Surely a short trot would do her good."

Chewing on a biscuit, Ebenezer thinks. "I haven't the time to ride her today, sister."

"I could ride her," I say sweetly.

"No, Betsy. Colonel Bouquet says there's Indian sign all around the ridges these days. I'll not have my Philadelphia sister's scalp hanging from a Shawnee lodge pole."

"I'll stay here, at the fort. I've not met anyone, nor even talked to anyone, save the Zanes, since coming home."

"You stay away from those soldiers, Betsy," Eb snaps. "Soldiers want only one thing from you."

"Ebenezer," Aunt Bessie scolds, "your sister looks so wan this morning, so pale and listless." She gives me a wink, so quicklike I'm not sure I really saw it. "Surely a short trot would do Betsy some good, too."

"The shortest of trots, then. Betsy, be sure to stay—"

Rachel Johnson runs for cover as I bolt from the table. Under my skirt I'm wearing my knitted-silk *pantalons*.

I'm in the stable before my brother can change his mind.

"May," I whisper in her ear, "do you remember my promise? That I'd ride you, swifter than the wind, along the Ohio?"

The Merry May nods her head and nickers at me.

I saddle and bridle her in less time than it takes to sneeze.

As I lead her out, the Merry May snorts and scrapes at the ground. Eb, Jonathan, and Silas come up fast, their arms outstretched to stop me. I swing my right leg over the saddle.

"Betsy!" Eb shouts. "I thought you meant Maybelle! The Merry May is much too spirited—"

"I shan't be long!" I shout, settling my feet into the stirrups. The Merry May snorts again and wheels away from Eb as he snatches at the reins. I touch my right heel to her flank. She takes off at a gallop.

"Sister, I forbid you—"

I lean far back in the saddle, my stirruped boots almost out in front of me, as we canter down the steep hill to the dock. I nudge the Merry May onto the river trail and away from Fort Henry.

May likes to step out. That means she'd rather trot than walk, gallop than canter. I like to step out, too. After my fortnight's confinement under Eb's thumb, I'm ready to burst with pent-up energy. I want to ride and ride until my heart is pounding in my throat.

Freedom!

We gallop down the river trail, the Merry May's hooves pounding the trail. I move with her. Horse and rider are one: As her neck shoots forward at every stride, my hands follow the reins to encourage her to run her fastest.

We jump over a log on the trail, the wind whistling in my ears. In a glade a herd of deer bolts out of our way. My fingers fold around the Merry May's mane as we warp and weave, back and forth on the winding trail. I almost forget to breathe. Spiderwebs brush my face. Branches pull at my long hair.

With a burst of speed the Merry May charges up a hill. Almost at the top I say, "Whoa, girl," and pull her down to a stop.

Far below us the Ohio glimmers like quicksilver. A fiery quilt of autumn hills dips and rolls into the distance.

I feel the Merry May panting between my knees. She gives off as much heat as a hearth fire.

"We're home, May," I whisper, patting her sweaty neck. At last Philadelphia melts away, like a knob of butter on warm bread. This is me, the wilderness. The trees, the hills, the river clean as melted snow. I've ridden for miles and not seen another person. I've thought about Philadelphia often these past weeks, especially Great-Aunt Elizabeth and my friends, but surely God set aside this country for the Zanes!

"My avaricious, overbearing brothers will not ruin my homecoming. They have no more idea as to how a Philadelphia lady is supposed to behave than you do, May. With the proper deportment, I can do as I please. Isn't that right, girl?"

The Merry May rolls her eyes toward me and stays silent.

I dismount to let her rest for a bit. When her flanks stop heaving, I lead her down the other side of the hill and to the riverbank for a drink. A cool breeze off the river dries the sweat on my neck and temples. I lift my hair and become cooler still.

"Just a few sips of water, May. You'll have the whole trough back at the fort. I don't want you chilled."

While my mare sips, I kneel upstream and scoop water from the river to slake my own thirst. I'm just about to remount when I see a log in the river coming toward us.

Something about it strikes me as odd. It does not float along with the current but pushes hard against it. I see a bit of a splash behind the log as it lurches forward. It lurches forward again, and this time I see feet kicking at the water.

Feet.

A chill shudders through me. I lead the Merry May behind a tree and peep around it.

The log is now downriver and far enough away for me to spy a man clinging to one side. He has long black hair and is dressed in buckskins. He has no weapons that I can see: no musket, no powder horn in his belt, not even a knife.

The man shambles out of the water and collapses against a sandbar, his face turned toward the sun. He's pale with exhaustion—*not a Shawnee*—and there's blood on his tunic.

The Merry May and I watch his labored breathing. She gives me a nudge with her nose and nickers softly in my ear.

"He needs help, May. I won't be a moment."

I wrap her reins around a tree branch and creep slowly toward the man.

"Do you need assistance, sir?" I call out. "May I accompany you to safety? I have a mount waiting."

The man smiles as he turns his face toward me.

"This is the Virginia shore of the Ohio River, and my name is Betsy Zane, sir. I live at Zane Station, close to Fort Henry."

The man struggles to his elbows. "Betsy? It's Isaac."

"Isaac Zane?"

My brother's skin is as pale as mine with my rice powder, but his pallor is real. His lips are blue and his teeth are chattering.

"Why are you here?" we ask together. Isaac groans and lies down again. "Betsy, help . . . help me," he gasps.

"We'll go home," I say. "Eb, Aunt Bessie, Jonathan, Silas, Andrew—we're all home."

I help him to his feet. He is wet, dead weight against me.

A bit of fresh blood stains the upper portion of his tunic.

"You've been shot?" I cry out. "Tomahawked?"

Isaac tucks one side of his mouth into a smile. "Nothing so grand, Betsy. Pricker bushes, thorns . . . on the run. The Wyandot chasing me . . . all the way from Fort Detroit."

"Here's the Merry May. I'll give you a leg up."

It takes several tries to hoist Isaac into the saddle. The Merry May, her nostrils wide, shies away from me. Her questioning brown eyes are so wide, I can see the whites.

"Easy, May," I say, stroking her neck. "It's just Isaac. We're going home."

"She smells my blood, Betsy," Isaac murmurs. "Blood always spooks horses."

"Hold on tightly. We must ascend this hill. Isn't this extraordinary, the two us meeting here?"

"I always cross here: the sandbar, the shallows, the good cover." Isaac groans again. "No more talking, Betsy. I'd like to try and get some sleep."

Returning home takes ages. I have to hold my mare back, because she wants to charge forward at every step. She's terrified of Isaac's scent and tries to buck him off. Whenever her back legs begin to bunch underneath her, I have to hold my crop against her hindquarters.

"May," I say firmly, "no bucking. Easy, girl."

Of course I'm glad to see Isaac, but I'm gladder still to have found him when I did. Eb won't dare be cross with me now.

I whisper to the Merry May all the way home. Despite her prancing, Isaac has fallen asleep, his face against her left wither, her mane twisted around his fingers.

While Isaac sleeps, I watch the Ohio and the river trail for Wyandot.

The sun looks to be about noon when I see Fort Henry. Eb and Jonathan pace back and forth in front of the main gate. When they see me, they begin to run down the hill.

Stop running, you fools. You'll scare the Merry May and she'll buck Isaac clear to Pittsburgh.

To their credit my brothers do stop running when they see the burden on May's back.

"A settler?" Eb asks. "Shot off a flatboat?"

"It's Isaac," I reply. "He's escaped from the Wyandot again."

For the rest of the day Aunt Bessie sets me to fetching comforts for Isaac. Comfrey roots to bind his wounds, buckeye and chamomile tea to soothe his spirit and encourage sleep. I fetch soap, towels, blankets, bandages. I hold the soup bowl in my hands as Aunt Bessie spoons warm venison broth into his mouth.

As Isaac sleeps, he has fitful dreams and mutters strange words and epithets. He says her name, "Myeerah, Myeerah," again and again as tears roll down his cheeks.

The rest of us glance at one another uneasily as Isaac's heathen intentions fill the Virginia Zane House. Isaac's wrists and elbows jerk and twitch. Surely my brother must be dreaming of holding his Wyandot princess in his arms, mourning a love that can never be.

Isaac sleeps round the clock. The next afternoon the two of us sit before the fire, my brother lost in his own thoughts. His Wyandot buckskins have been burned. Mostly he's wearing bandages and Great-Aunt Elizabeth's Persian Pears and Pine Cones quilt around his bare shoulders. He has the same dark hair and eyes as the rest of us.

"You're not eating your Sally Lunn," I say, pointing to a teacake at his elbow. "I made it myself."

"You made this?" he asks in mock surprise.

"Isaac, you know I did! Rachel would never serve anything so lumpy and burnt."

Isaac lifts the plate from the side table. He takes a bite from a part of my teacake that isn't singed black. "Delicious, Betsy."

I watch him take another bite of scorched teacake, then another. He must be half starved.

"How long have I been here?" he asks.

"Since noon yesterday. You've been sleeping and dreaming . . . dreaming a lot."

"Have I?"

"You called out her name, Myeerah, again and again."

Isaac says nothing and stares at the hearth fire. Tears well up in his eyes.

"You must love her very much," I say softly.

"We're married, Betsy," he whispers.

"Married?" I say, shocked to my bones.

"According to the Wyandot we are."

"Does that . . . count?"

"To us it does."

Isaac looks at me. "I haven't seen you since you were a little girl in pinafores and pigtails. When did you return to us?"

"A little less than two weeks ago."

"Do you miss Philadelphia?"

"My friends. Great-Aunt Elizabeth. I've spent almost half my life living in Philadelphia. It will always be a part of me."

"Betsy, I'm twenty-six years old, and I've spent more

than half my life among the Wyandot." He looks at me warily. "Myeerah and I have two children."

I swallow hard. "Children?"

"Two fine boys. Princes. When I'm with Myeerah, all I think about is Zane Station. When I'm here, all I think about is her."

I have no words of comfort for him. In the firelight the pluming steam from the teakettle looks for all the world like a red-and-orange feather.

"I'll make you some tea, Isaac."

As the tea steeps, we fall silent again. I hear the *thump, thump, thump* of soldiers' footsteps at their drill. The hearth fire whispers and glows. The Merry May kicks the walls of her stall.

"This is rose-hip tea," I say, pouring out a steaming cup. "A woman in Pittsburgh told me this tea wards off sickness. Aunt Bessie has been giving you chamomile and venison broth and such. Maybe this will help, too."

Isaac takes an eager pull from his teacup and swallows in a hurry. He coughs. "A bit tart, wouldn't you say, sister?"

"Really? I haven't tried it yet."

He places the cup of bitter tea next to the burnt Sally Lunn. "It's good to be home," my brother says softly.

The Merry May kicks against her stall again.

"Uh . . . I've been looking for a chance to ride the Merry May all day," I say. "Will you be all right? Sitting before the fire?"

"Of course I will, Betsy. You ride your mare—she's a good horse. Don't worry about me."

As I leave him, my brother leans forward a bit toward the fire. Great-Aunt Elizabeth's quilt slides off his bare right shoulder. Isaac's left side is covered with the quilt. His right side is covered with Wyandot tattoos.

I take the Merry May for a long ride. I collect the reins and pace her at an easy trot this time, because I want to think.

I ride well beyond where I found Isaac. I ride until the trail is gone; we stop at the very edge of the wilderness. I smell no cook smoke, no lye soap. I see no cabins on the ridges, no cleared newground. I hear no *clink* of metal against metal. Except for the constant bird song, all I hear is the soothing creak of saddle leather and my breathing in time with the Merry May's.

An oak, big around as a small cabin, stands in my way. Beyond it is another oak and another. The Ohio Company of the Commonwealth of Virginia's trail has ended. Surely it picks up again near Fort Randolph, but for now I might as well be the only person on earth.

I dismount and sit with my back against the tree. The Merry May gives herself a good shake, then crops the fodder. The sweet smell of clover fills the air.

"Oh, May," I murmur to her. "It would be so romantic, just like *Romeo and Juliet*, if only the main characters weren't Isaac and Myeerah."

The Philadelphia Quakers forbid theatrical entertainments. My girlfriends and I were obliged to read aloud Mr. Shakespeare's plays in Great-Aunt Elizabeth's parlor, acting out the parts in grand style. If it was my turn to play lovesick Romeo, or melancholy Hamlet, or good King Hal, I'd wear Great-Great-Grandfather Karl's helmet and armor, his blunderbuss clanking against the silvered, crenellated breastplate.

"May, Romeo's and Juliet's families, the Montagues and Capulets, had no reason to dislike each other. Hate and distrust had become a habit, nothing more."

The Merry May snorts a bit in reply and keeps on chewing.

I stand up, gather the reins, and step into the left stirrup.

"Good girl," I say as she stands perfectly still while I swing my right leg over. No sidesaddle for me.

"Walk on, May."

Surely there are those among the Wyandot who are as affronted by the Zanes as the Zanes are affronted by the Wyandot. But why are we all so insulted? We've done nothing to hurt the Wyandot, nor have they hurt us. Our enmities are a habit, nothing more.

Isaac has a wife and children who need him. He should be with his family.

"The Montagues and Capulets learned too late, May, the sort of grief that hating out of habit will bring. It's not too late for the Zanes, and I hope not too late for the Wyandot. Isaac belongs with his family. He's my brother and he'll always be a Zane, but he's just like a settler who decides to take his family upriver or down. We'll see him again someday."

Once the trail evens out, we trot, canter, then gallop home.

Back at Zane Station I pull the Merry May down to a stop. Aunt Bessie, Eb, Jonathan, Andrew, and Silas are standing on the dock. My brothers are scowling and staring hard at the river. Andrew points to the far riverbank. He, Eb, and Silas look sharply, then shake their heads.

Aunt Bessie is crying into her apron. Her little ones look up at her in terror.

"What's wrong, Eb?" I ask, dismounting.

Eb glares at me. "Why weren't you watching him? We left him with you."

"Who?" I look into all their faces. "No . . . Isaac's gone? The Wyandot were here? They captured him again?"

"Captured, my foot," Eb sputters. "He took my best buckskins and a side of smoked venison. He's been lying to us, Betsy. Lying to his family for all these years." He points to the Ohio side. "He wants to be with *them*."

"What did he say to you, Betsy?" Aunt Bessie asks. "You two had your heads together all afternoon."

"He's married," I say shortly, "with two sons."

Eb cups his hands around his lips. "You are not my brother! Do you hear me, Isaac? We do not have a brother named Isaac!"

"I have a brother named Isaac," I announce. "Don't you see, Eb? They're just like Romeo and Juliet. We shouldn't—"

"Put your horse away," Eb says in a voice as quiet and deadly as a copperhead. "The Zanes do not have a brother named Isaac."

The river gurgles, as though in laughter.

8

Juledag

"We've written out our letters, and our numbers through twenty. Won't you tell us about Christmas in Philadelphia again, please, Aunt Betsy!" Sarah pleads.

"Yes, please, Aunt Betsy," Elizabeth echoes. "We've been ever so good today, haven't we?"

"Yvonne and Stephen haven't written out their letters," I reply. "Stephen? I'll help you if need be."

Our hornbook is a slab of gray slate propped on a chair. Our quill pens are lumps of charcoal from the hearth. Our schoolhouse is the southeast corner of the ground floor of Zane House, lit up in the morning sun. I am the schoolmistress, with five years at a Quaker girls' school to my name.

It was Aunt Bessie who suggested the schoolhouse, although I'm not sure whether it was her children's education or her own freedom she longed for.

Seven-year-old Stephen Bouquet, son of Fort Henry's Colonel Bouquet, squeezes his lump of charcoal so hard that it bursts into a little black cloud about his hand.

"Please tell us about the Christmas food again," he begs. "I'm tired of venison and cornbread."

"Tell about feeding the birds!" his ten-year-old sister, Yvonne, joins in. "Feeding the birds for Christmas!"

"If you two promise to write out your letters," I say, "and your numbers." They nod eagerly.

"All right, then. Most of the leading citizens of Philadelphia are Quakers and celebrate no Christmas whatever," I begin. "Great-Aunt Elizabeth and I felt sorry for them December after December. I can't imagine the long winter without *Juledag* to relieve the dreariness."

"*Juledag* means Christmas," Stephen whispers loudly to his sister. "*Noël.*"

"That's right, Christmas Day," I correct gently. "Stephen, what language does the word *Juledag* come from?"

Stephen turns scarlet and stares at the floor.

"Danish," I say. "The Zanes are from Denmark."

"Papa is from Switzerland," Yvonne announces. "*Noël* means Christmas in French."

"Thank you, Yvonne. Just as they do in Denmark, on December first I would start feeding the birds. I'd hang birdseed cakes, made of rendered suet and sunflower seeds, and strings of popcorn on the trees and fences. Later in the month Young Sam would help me tie sheaves of wheat on the stable roof."

"Young Sam is a slave," Sarah interrupts.

"He's a soldier now," I correct gently. "Then I'd choose the reddest apples I could find, string them together with red ribbon, pine cones, and pine branches, and hang them above the front door. By New Year's Day the birds, squirrels, and chipmunks would have nibbled the apples down to nothing. Not even the seeds would be left."

"I feed the birds, too," Yvonne says.

"Do not," Stephen says indignantly.

"Do, too! I toss them bits of Mama's cornbread when she's not looking."

"Mama's cornbread is for the soldiers!" Stephen shouts.

"The birds are hungry, too," Yvonne replies.

"Not as hungry as soldiers!" Stephen shouts again.

"Food," I say. Stephen falls silent. "On market Mondays Old Bess, Great-Aunt Elizabeth, and I would poke about the German stalls looking for Scandinavian spices and condiments. Little sacks of cardamon, cinnamon, allspice, nutmeg, citron, almonds, and raisins would pile up in the kitchen, giving the whole house a wonderful fragrance."

"Aunt Betsy," Elizabeth interrupts, frowning, "is Old Bess a soldier now, too?"

"Girls can't be soldiers," Stephen says, sneeringly.

"Stephen, would you prefer to copy letters?" I ask.

Silence.

"A week before Christmas Old Bess would open the kitchen windows a crack, fire up the oven, and begin baking. She made almond cakes and *æblekage*, an apple cake with cinnamon, cardamon, and cloves."

Stephen sighs. "Cake's my favorite."

"You're too little to remember cake," Yvonne scolds.

"How could anyone forget cake?" I ask.

Stephen grins at me.

"Our glum next-door neighbors, the Fryes, would just happen to drop by after the cakes were out of the oven. 'Would the Misses Zane be interested in buying some chickens?' Mr. Frye would ask.

"All eight Fryes would linger in the parlor, smelling the heavenly scent of *æblekage* warm from the oven.

"Of course, Great-Aunt Elizabeth would pass around steaming slices of *æblekage* dressed with whipped cream and raspberry jam. Of course, all eight Fryes would gobble down every crumb.

"She would press Mr. and Mrs. Frye into taking just a wee dram of Cherry Heering—with four or five refills apiece! Mr. Frye would start telling funny stories, with Mrs. Frye stomping her feet and wiping her eyes, she was laughing so hard."

My students giggle. "Drunk!" Stephen whispers.

"The next morning a cage, three dazed and shivering chickens within it, would be perched on the back stoop.

"'Not a Christmas gift,' Great-Aunt Elizabeth would say with a merry laugh. 'These chickens are strictly business.'

"Those were good times," I say softly. *She was right—we did give those Quakers a fair bit of gossip for round the tea table. Great-Aunt Elizabeth always made Christmas so much fun.*

"On the morning of Christmas Eve Old Bess would bake cutout butter cookies: dozens of bears, hearts, wreaths, ponies, and *Jule Nisse* (whom the Dutch call Sint Nicholaas).

"On Christmas morning, she'd stuff a goose with *medisterpøse*, pork sausage with chopped apples and chestnuts. By noon half of Philadelphia was scented with the delicious aroma of roasting goose.

"Our *Julenkage*—Christmas cake—was bursting with marzipan, that's almond paste, and hazelnuts, candied fruit, and citron. It was topped with sweetened whipped cream."

"When would you eat the cookies?" Stephen asks.

I shrug my shoulders. "Whenever we were hungry, I reckon."

Stephen sighs again. "Three kinds of cake . . . *and* cookies."

"Then on Christmas night Great-Aunt Elizabeth and I would stand in the front yard, even in heavy snow, and sing our favorite Danish carol at the tops of our voices:

Et barn er født i Betlehem, Betlehem.
Thi glaede sig Jerusalem! Halleluja! Halleluja!

We'd sing in English too:

A child was born in Bethlehem, Bethlehem.
Sing a glad song, Jerusalem! Hallelujah! Hallelujah!

"I'd sing the glad word again and again. 'Glaede. Glaede. You're supposed to be glad, Philadelphia!' I'd shout until the neighborhood dogs began to bark.

"We'd go to church and listen to the congregation sing German carols. *Vom Himmel hoch, Es ist ein' Ros,* and *Warum stollt ich* filled the frosty, candlelit air."

"It all sounds so wonderful." Elizabeth sighs. "I wish we were in Philadelphia for Christmas."

I look at her in amazement. "And miss Christmas in the wilderness? We'll have a proper Zane *Juledag*. You'll see."

Aunt Bessie, who was a McCullough before she married, grew up in New Hampshire. Apparently, New Englanders celebrate Christmas with as little cheer as Philadelphians, for she has brought no customs west with her. She is more than happy to enjoy December and *Juledag* our way.

Just as in Philadelphia *and* in Denmark, on December first we begin to feed the birds. I hang long garlands of popcorn on the pine trees. Aunt Bessie melts tallow in the candle-making tub. When the tallow cools a bit, I pour seeds into the tub and mix it with my hands. I shape the seed cakes into hearts, horses, and stars.

Elizabeth, Sarah, and Noah are allowed to stay up late and help me make the seed cakes. Noah's horses look like lumpy cows. We let the seed cakes harden overnight.

We use grapevine to hang some of them on the trees, and save the rest for later in the month. All through December the wrens, redbirds, chickadees, blue jays, nuthatches, and tufted titmice will fly from tree to tree enjoying their Christmas favors. Their joyous singing already fills our ears from sunrise to sunset.

We have no wheat sheaves to hang over the stable doorway for the birds. My brothers help me tie cornstalks together. I bind peeled ears to the stalks and hang them above the stable doors instead. The birds don't seem to mind.

In mid-December we Zanes linger at the breakfast table with Colonel Henry Bouquet. Jonathan, Silas, Andrew, and Eb are leaning back in their chairs, their arms folded across their chests.

"General Washington's army will have to wait, and so will the Shawnee," Eb says to Colonel Bouquet. "Christmas is one week away, Colonel, and that holiday is something special among the Zanes, especially with our sister home."

Colonel Bouquet says, "There are no better scouts on the frontier than the Zane brothers. Thanks be to God that General Cornwallis surrendered his army to General Washington just two months ago. But Cornwallis said nothing about surrendering forts in these western territories. The enemy will defend Fort Niagara, Fort Michilimackinac, Fort Augustus on Green Bay, Fort Detroit, and Fort Kaskaskia on the Mississippi River at all costs.

"There're not enough American forts to defend the Ohio Valley; surely the British will try to push us east, into surrendered territory.

"King George will use local tribes, and his Rangers have been trained in forest fighting for these purposes. Fort Henry needs the Zanes to look for war parties and signs of settlement raids."

"We'd be gone for weeks," Jonathan replies.

"Colonels William Crawford and David Williamson from Fort Pitt have already been here," Silas says. "We turned them down, too."

"Your sausage is wonderful, Mrs. Zane. *C'est magnifique*," Colonel Bouquet says in his peculiar Swiss accent. "But your husband? *Les indiens* have been so quiet since the summer. Someday our luck will change, no? Especially with the war over in the east. Perhaps, Mrs. Zane, you could persuade your husband."

Aunt Bessie shakes her head. "The harder Eb is pushed, the harder he pushes back. And the Zanes dearly love Christmas."

Eb, Silas, Jonathan, and Andrew nod their heads in unison. My brothers have all sprouted facial hair for the winter. Their dark beards and mustaches, their dark eyes, make them look more like lanky bears than people.

"If you were in the army, I could order you to go," Colonel Bouquet grumbles.

"That's why we're not," Jonathan snaps.

"Right," Silas mumbles around a mouthful of sausage. Andrew nods his head again.

Colonel Ebenezer Zane, of the 3rd Virginia, clears his throat. "I can't, *I won't* cross the river without my brothers, even with an army commission. You know that, Henry. It'll have to be after the new year."

Colonel Bouquet quickly eats his share of the sausage, stands up, clicks his heels, bows to us ladies, and leaves the house.

———————

There is no saffron, no cardamon, no cinnamon, dill, or caraway, no almonds or citron, and no beer here in the wilderness. But we make do. Jonathan has shot some wild turkeys, and Andrew has trapped some rabbits. Rachel Johnson makes a dressing of cornbread, apples, and black walnuts, which we've been eating with the roasted turkey since the first day of Advent. Her stuffing is not as good as Old Bess's, but of course I won't tell her that.

Candles are much too scarce to burn on the windowsills all evening, even for Advent. I watch the glowing logs in the hearth and pretend they're candles.

One tradition I'd forgotten is the sunset gift. During Advent everyone gets a little present every evening after supper: a lump of maple sugar, a corncob pipe, a cornhusk doll, a twist of homespun yarn, a wool pen wiper, a short stack of writing paper and homemade ink. We take turns being the present giver.

Silas made the mistake of giving Noah a whistle made from an old rifle barrel. Now Noah blows his whistle from sunrise to sunset.

On Christmas Eve the real presents appear. Ebenezer has made his children a toboggan. I give Aunt Bessie one of Great-Aunt Elizabeth's velvet bonnets, only a bit crushed from the journey west. I give my brothers deerskin hats I've made, with a bit of beadwork on the turned-up brims.

I receive more maple sugar, stockings, both new and repaired, a new set of horseshoes for the Merry May, and an indigo shawl Aunt Bessie made herself.

Silas and Jonathan have made an oak frame for Great-Great-Grandfather Karl's portrait.

"When can we use the toboggan, Pa?" Sarah asks, jumping up and down in excitement.

"'Boggan, 'boggan, 'boggan," Noah shouts, jumping up and down in unison with his sister.

Eb peers out the window. "You may all ride tomorrow morning, if the weather holds."

This Christmas Eve it snows so hard, I can't see the stable. We wake up to blue sky and a thick blanket of sparkling snow.

Elizabeth, Sarah, Noah, and I wolf down our sausage gravy and biscuits. We gobble down the precious eggs the Van Swearingens gave us for Christmas.

Aunt Bessie bundles us up against the cold.

Eb has waxed the toboggan's runners to a fine gloss.

I'm supposed to be taking care of my nieces and nephew, but on the toboggan the four of us fly down the hill toward the river, me screaming just as loudly as the children. We roll off into a soft drift at the last moment so as not to plunge into the flooded Ohio. Lucky for us the toboggan skitters off into a snowbank. I find a rope in the stable and fasten one end to my wrist, the other end to the toboggan.

On our fifth trudge up the hill, I notice four sentries at the main gate of Fort Henry watching us closely.

"*God Jul*—that means Merry Christmas," I call out to them. "Would you care for a ride on our new toboggan?"

"Merry Christmas and thank you, miss," one of them calls back. "But we're on duty. We can't leave our posts."

"We'll guard Fort Henry for you. One ride can't hurt.

Just be sure to hold fast to our new toboggan. See? I've tied it to my wrist, but I'll untie it for you. Just one quick ride."

The sentries regard each other. Quickly, one sentry gives me his musket. The others lean theirs against the fortress wall.

In front of my eyes these steadfast soldiers turn into riotous boys. With great whoops and hollers they slide down the hill toward the Ohio River.

"Be sure to roll off!" I call down to them. Two sentries roll to the left, two roll to the right. By the time they're up the hill again, more soldiers have come out of the fort.

Elizabeth, Sarah, and I hold muskets as the soldiers take turns racing down the hill. Even little Noah is holding a musket, which makes me nervous until I shake the powder and shot out of it. With our shoulders back and our spines stiff, we march back and forth this Christmas morning, pretending to be soldiers, while the soldiers pretend to be us.

Fifteen soldiers are tobogganing and having snowball fights when Aunt Bessie calls us home for Christmas dinner. Sarah and I are putting the toboggan away in the stable when I see Colonel Bouquet scowling and marching out of the main gate.

In preparation for dinner, I change out of my wet clothes and into dry ones just as quickly as I can. I decide to wear my brand-new stockings and a chemise I haven't worn since Philadelphia.

One dress I did *not* abandon, in my haste to leave last summer, was my velvet gown. Great-Aunt Elizabeth traded a Pineapple Medallion and Palmapores quilt for an entire bolt of pre-War French velvet, the color of claret. Our dressmaker gave it the deepest flounce I've ever seen, and huge, old-fashioned puffed sleeves. I pretend it's a gown the Princess Elizabeth wore, before her reign as queen.

I look into the mirror, which is hanging from a hook in the bedroom wall. After this morning's exertions, my cheeks are almost as red as the gown. My black eyes sparkle as I brush my hair and fasten it up with tortoiseshell hairpins. I tie a black ribbon in my hair. I find the Baltic-amber earbobs and the pearl necklace from Great-Aunt Elizabeth's jewel box and put those on, too.

My stomach growls as delicious scents float up the staircase.

We sit down to a fine Christmas dinner. It's a far cry from a Danish *Juledag* feast, but we're Americans now and we should celebrate accordingly, I reckon. We eat roast turkey, with cornbread-and-chestnut dressing, squash, succotash, and cherry-cranberry pie.

We gather round the burning Yule log after dinner.

"Sing that Danish carol, Betsy," Jonathan asks me. "Do you remember it? The glad song."

"Great-Aunt Elizabeth and I used to sing the glad song. Do you remember the English, Jonathan?"

"I believe I do."

We both stand up. I begin to sing:

*"Et barn er født i Betlehem, Betlehem.
Thi glaede sig Jerusalem! Halleluja! Halleluja!"*

108

Then Jonathan sings:

"A child was born in Bethlehem, Bethlehem.
Sing a glad song, Jerusalem! Hallelujah! Hallelujah!"

"Glaede," I say. "Glad. That's my favorite Danish word."
"It suits you," Aunt Bessie says, smiling at me.
Then Jonathan sings:

Den yndigste rose er funden,
blandt stiveste torne oprunden.
Vor Jesus, den dejligste pode,
blandt syndige mennesker gro'de.

"The rose hymn! How can you remember it?" Silas asks.
"Our father used to sing that one before you were born,
Betsy," Jonathan explains. "Something about the loveliest
rose was found among the stiffest thorns."
Eb pats his stomach. "A fine dinner. And fine singing
as well. You have a better memory than I have, Jonathan."
"I've never thought about it before," I say, "but didn't
our father look like Great-Great-Grandfather Karl? Look
at the portrait."
All eyes turn to the portrait in its brand-new frame,
hanging in pride of place above the mantelpiece. I remember our father having the same dark hair, the same dark
eyes. All our skins have that same rosy glow.
"All you Zanes look alike," Aunt Bessie says.
"Extraordinary."

We sit in silence for a moment. I close my eyes. I can almost see my mother before me. I can almost feel her soft lips brushing my forehead as she used to kiss me good night.

Eb says, "If you ladies will excuse us."

All my brothers pick up their muskets. I know they're going into the woods to relieve themselves, even though we have a chamber pot under each bed. Little Noah follows the Zane men out the front door, a self-important swagger to his backside.

I hear Old Sam and Rachel having their Christmas dinner in the kitchen. They live in a shack close to the stable; Old Sam hardly ever comes into Zane House. I wonder if he thinks about Old Bess, if he would like to meet his son, Young Sam, someday.

Old Sam is from Philadelphia, too, but he's not free because my father decided the Zanes needed him in Virginia. He's lost the son he never set eyes on, his wife, and his chance for freedom.

If I were Old Sam, I'd be too bitter to think straight.

I stand in the kitchen doorway. "*God Jul*—that means Merry Christmas, Old Sam. Rachel."

"Thank you, Miss Betsy," Old Sam says politely, but with no expression in his voice.

"Young Sam is in General Washington's army. But then, you already know that," I say in a forced and sprightly tone.

Old Sam just nods and forks turkey into his mouth. Rachel pats his hand.

What a sad thing it must be, I think suddenly, *to live in a country that puts such stock in liberty, only to know you'll be having none of it.*

"Well, a Merry Christmas to you both," I say stiffly.

When my brothers return, Eb is frowning and holding tightly to Noah's hand. Silas, Jonathan, and Andrew lean their muskets near the windows.

"Let's have a bit of Christmas cheer before the fire," Aunt Bessie says.

We all sit before the roaring Yule log, drinking rose-hip tea spiked with Jonathan's applejack.

"This has been a fine day," Aunt Bessie says softly. "What were the New Hampshire McCulloughs thinking, not celebrating Christmas?"

"Fine indeed. Betsy," Eb says, turning to me, "did any soldiers follow you home this morning? Any sentries?"

"No."

"You're sure of that? Think carefully now."

"I'm sure. Colonel Bouquet came out of the main gate to see what all the rumpus was about. He ordered the soldiers to return to the fort."

"What is it, Eb?" Aunt Bessie asks.

Noah has fallen asleep by the fire. Sarah is nodding and sinking lower and lower into her brand-new rocking chair. Elizabeth is leaning against her mother's arm, trying to stay awake.

"Put the little ones to bed, Bess. We'll talk after."

It's full dark outside when Aunt Bessie returns.

"On the river porch," Ebenezer says, "we saw footprints in the snow, a lot of them, especially by the window. Somebody has been spying on us this Christmas Day. Somebody with cold feet, for he kept moving, stomping his feet in the snow to keep them warm."

"Shawnee!" Aunt Bessie whispers.

"It's Isaac!" I shout. "He's come home for Christmas!"

"It wasn't Isaac, sister—these tracks are too small. And moccasins they were, not a soldier's boots," Eb replies.

"That doesn't tell us anything," Silas argues. "These soldiers are lucky to have any shoes at all."

"You'd think the Indians would leave us alone, on this day of all days," Aunt Bessie says angrily.

"This is precisely the day they would attack," Andrew replies. "We looked all around the house and saw only the one set of prints. We would have tracked him into the woods but for Noah."

"Thank you for that," Aunt Bessie says.

"We'll follow the tracks tomorrow, in full daylight," Silas adds, nodding to Jonathan and Andrew.

"I'm not going to let a busybody ruin my Christmas," I say. I take a sip from my applejack tea.

Silas stands up. "Here's to you, Betsy, and to your first Christmas home again. You've kept your Zane spirit and the Virginia Zane House is the merrier for it. You are a rose among thorns. *Skål.*"

Jonathan, Andrew, and Eb stand up, too. *"Skål,"* they say together.

Aunt Bessie says, "To *Juledag.*"

9

Lost in the Hay

Surely Isaac will come home today. It is my thirteenth March twenty-fifth and my very first Lady's Day. This fourth day of spring dawns clear and fresh, with a flower-scented breeze blowing up from the Shenandoah. Leaflets cover the laurel branches in a cheerful green mist. Tender grass shoots poke up from the mud.

Lady's Day is spent receiving presents and planting flowers and flowering bushes. I'll plant Aunt Bessie's rose-bush today. My present to myself is cleaning my saddles and tack, for the riding season has begun.

After breakfast Aunt Bessie and Eb give me a woolen scarf and mittens, dyed to match in deep rose. Silas sets a bear cub he'd whittled out of white pine next to my plate. Jonathan gives me a wax jar shaped like a beehive and full of honey to sweeten my rose-hip tea. Andrew gives me a bird carved out of pipestem clay.

"This is for you, Aunt Bessie," I say. I hold in my palm the little alabaster elephant Karl Zane brought all the way from Denmark. "It's the symbol of the Danish Crown. Look, the tusks and the blanket on its back are pure gold."

"Gold?" Jonathan says. He, Andrew, and Silas lean across the table for a better look.

"Why, thank you, Betsy," Aunt Bessie says. "You'll look mighty fetching in that scarf and mittens for the ball on Saturday night. Rose suits your coloring."

"My sister does not need to fetch a husband," Eb growls around a mouthful of venison, "especially a soldier. I'll remind you that she's only thirteen."

"I'll be fourteen in June," I say. "I'm not a child."

Eb shakes his spoon at me. "No sister of mine is going to marry a soldier." As he scolds, his voice becomes louder and louder. "She'll not spend her life washing bloody bandages, following a camp full of randy soldiers, and having babies in an army tent."

"Ebenezer Zane, you watch your tongue," Aunt Bessie snaps.

"As long as this is my house—" Eb shouts back.

"This is *our* house!" Jonathan yells above them both. Silas and Andrew stand up so quickly, their chairs tip over.

"I don't want to be married!" I scream.

Silence. They all look at me.

"Why ever not?" Aunt Bessie asks after a moment.

"Maybelle and the Merry May would be too jealous," I say, helping myself to more spiced crabapples.

After tonight's supper Andrew pounds a lively beat on the floor with a log while Aunt Bessie teaches me dance steps.

114

We promenade, jig, sashay, do-si-do, and allemande left, far into the night.

"You'll wear me out, child," she pants. She collapses on the bench farthest from the fire, fanning herself with her hands.

"Aunt Bessie, you haven't taught me how to swing yet."

"That's my favorite step." Jonathan bows at the waist. "Betsy, may I have this dance?"

"Remember to curtsey before saying yes," Aunt Bessie calls out. "And look a bit undecided before the curtsey. It keeps the men on their toes."

Andrew pounds the beat faster and faster while Jonathan swings me so hard, I get dizzy. My feet knock against the flour barrel.

"You're a good dancer, Betsy," Jonathan says, gasping for breath when we stop. "You'll fetch a husband soon enough."

"I just came home. The last thing I want is a husband who will take me away from Zane Station."

Later I'm too excited about Saturday's ball to fall asleep. I toss and turn in my bed half the night. Then my sore dancer's feet remind me of Isaac, who did not come home for Lady's Day.

The next morning, I try on my velvet gown. I've grown taller since Christmas; my best dress shows far too much of a lady's ankle. I have to let out the hem to lengthen the skirt. I have to let out the bodice, too, I'm proud to say.

Aunt Bessie, who is a much better needlewoman than I'll ever be, adds panels of white lace to the bodice seams.

This Saturday before Easter dawns cold. Leaden clouds hover so low and heavy, I imagine I could touch them. By midday, snowflakes the size of goose down fall heavy and wet on our hills. Wet snow blankets our fields, already turned up by Andrew and Maybelle for the spring planting. Snow covers the cabin and stable roofs.

Out in their brand-new paddock, Maybelle and the Merry May snort, kick, and spook at the snowflakes as if they'd never seen snow before.

Rachel hauls the tub into the kitchen after supper. I brought three bars of French soap with me from Philadelphia, all scented with lemon verbena. With one pitcher of hot water and one of cold, I stand in the tub and take a quick sponge bath with one of my precious soaps. My limbs shiver as the late storm blows cold wind and snow through the chinks in the log walls.

Clutching one of Great-Aunt Elizabeth's quilts, I run upstairs to change into my ball gown and most comfortable shoes. I pin up my hair and put on the Baltic-amber earbobs.

"How do I look?" I ask from the stairs, my heart pounding.

"Betsy, you're beautiful, a grown-up young lady!" Aunt Bessie exclaims. "You must be so excited, your first ball."

Downstairs I don my new mittens and Great-Aunt Elizabeth's black velvet cloak. I wrap my new scarf around my neck.

Silas escorts me to Fort Henry. Eb escorts Aunt Bessie.

The ball is held in the Officers' Mess, a long, low-ceilinged dining room with a fireplace at the far end. We pile our wraps onto a table near the door. I'm careful to tuck my new scarf and mittens within the folds of my cloak.

In the back of the Mess, benches have been lined up against the wall. Tables are crowded with punch bowls and cups, cakes, and custards. A tub of maple syrup stands ready to be drizzled on snowballs to refresh the dancers as they, and the music, heat up.

I count twenty soldiers. But there are only eight women: Aunt Bessie, the three Van Swearingen sisters, the three Clark sisters, and me. We won't be able to walk tomorrow. We'll have danced our feet clean off.

When our neighbor Peter Stalnaker picks up his fiddle, I'm already tapping my foot. Major John Linn balances a battered dulcimer on his lap. They practice a few bars of "Turkey in the Straw" and "The Brandywine Quickstep."

Eb holds a tin cup in the air as a cluster of soldiers stands around him. He pulls tiny strips of paper out of the cup and calls out names: "Cosby, Brown, Edwards, Baker, McWilliams, MacClean."

Six blushing soldiers stand to his right. The other soldiers cheer as the six tie aprons around their waists.

"The Grand Promenade," Peter Stalnaker, our caller, shouts. "Gents, choose your partners."

A soldier approaches me. Before I have a chance to look undecided prior to the curtsey, he wrenches my arm and me onto the dance floor.

I nod at the aproned soldiers and say, "So that's how it's done here in the wilderness. Those soldiers are women for the night, to even out the couples."

"Yer Miss Zane, ain't chee?" My partner grins down at me. Most of his teeth have rotted down to black stumps.

I just blink at him. The music begins.

"Stand your circle," Mr. Stalnaker shouts, "ladies on the right and gents on the left. Do-si-do your partner . . . do-si-do your corner . . . then, allemande left four times," he calls.

I remember to curtsey first before do-si-do-ing. We dancers are obliged to dodge children, who squeal and chase each other around the Officers' Mess like a pack of puppies.

I remember to hold out my left hand for the allemande left.

"One, two, three, four," I count, allemande lefting as grinning soldiers pass me by.

"Balance and swing . . . swing your new partner."

A new partner, thank goodness.

"The Grand Promenaaaaade," Mr. Stalnaker calls.

My new partner is Silas. "Fetch any husbands yet, Betsy?"

As we promenade round the ring, I give him a sharp elbow poke in the ribs. "You'll be the last to know."

"Second time, do-si-do your partner . . . do-si-do your corner . . . allemande left, four times. . . ."

I feel more confident this time. I even remember to smile and not count out loud.

Mr. Stalnaker calls out, "Swing, swing that purty little thing. . . ."

My new partner is a soldier I hadn't noticed before. His long, blond hair is clubbed with a black ribbon, but the dancing has mussed it a bit. Golden tendrils curl about his temples. He has the bluest eyes I've ever seen.

I can't stop looking into his eyes as we swing. He looks pleased and gives me a smile.

"How do you do?" he says. "My name is—"

"Do-si-do your partner. . . ."

I bump into him as we do-si-do. Our elbows knock together and spark off my funny bone.

He faces me again just as Mr. Stalnaker calls out, "Allemande left your partner. . . ."

That funny-bone feeling catches like a brushfire over me. I just stand there, hands at my sides, tingling all over and rooted to the floor. I hear, as if from a distance, faint music and the stomping of soldiers' boots.

"Miss Zane, your left hand?" he asks me.

He knows my name!

"W-what?" I hold out my right hand.

He smiles that smile again. Even, white teeth. "Miss Zane," he says, with a tilt to his head, "your other left hand?"

"Sorry," I try to say, but the word clogs in my throat.

By now four dance partners glare behind us.

He takes my left hand in his and gently pulls me behind him. Another soldier grabs my right hand. Allemande left-ing, I forget to count four soldiers and dance right by my

119

new partner. I watch the blond soldier dancing with Aunt Bessie. I don't know his name.

I watch him dance round the ring. He dances with each of the Clark sisters and Lucille Van Swearingen. Usually cool and smooth as custard, Lucille is blushing bright red.

"Once more round that ring!" Mr. Stalnaker shouts. The soldiers, even the ones wearing aprons, give a hearty cheer.

I'll be his partner again; he's four soldiers away.

As I dance, I rehearse what I'm going to say. This time I'll be ready. One soldier down, another, then another . . .

"Swing your new partner. . . ."

"My name is Elizabeth Zane," I say to him in a breathless voice. "But everyone has always called me Betsy."

He smiles and takes me into his arms. As we swing, I feel my heart pumping hard against his chest.

"My name is John McGlaughlin." He gives me that little tilt of the head again. His blue eyes shine.

I give him my best smile. "And what has everyone always called you, John McGlaughlin?"

We stop swinging. His smile turns to a puzzled frown. "John McGlaughlin," he replies. I stand there in horror, hoping the ground will open beneath my feet.

Betsy, what a stupid thing to ask! Now he'll never talk to you again—never, ever again!

As we do-si-do, I'm too embarrassed to look at him.

After the Grand Promenade is over, I flee to the refreshments. Mrs. Bouquet hands me a punch cup. I can hardly drink it, I'm trembling so hard. I slosh whiskey syllabub on the new lace panels of my dress.

"Oh, no!"

"Miss Zane, are you all right?" Mrs. Bouquet asks.

"My gown!" I open a side door and run outside, looking for clean snow. I put my cup down and rub snow onto my bodice, hoping it will dilute the whiskey stain. The snow feels good against my hot skin. I scoop up more snow and press it to my forehead.

What's the matter with you, Betsy? You're as jumpy as a spooked horse.

I take deep breaths. Near the east sally port some soldiers stand in a circle and pass a bottle among them; then they begin to sing:

Fare thee well, sweet Ireland, whom I shall see no more.
My heart is almost bleeding, to leave my native shore.
But the king, he has commanded, so we must sail away,
To fight the Sons of Liberty, far from Ballykay.

I gulp down the rest of my whiskey syllabub, hoping my heart will stop racing. Mrs. Bouquet has not been frugal with the whiskey; my innards feel on fire.

"Miss Zane, I'm very sorry if I've disconcerted you."

It's him!

I take an extra-deep breath and turn slowly round. The snow clouds have blown away. The moon is full. A halo of moonlight shines behind him, turning his blond hair to silver.

"I'm quite all right, Mr. McGlaughlin. It's so warm in the Mess with the fire. And all the dancers."

"Actually, it's Lieutenant McGlaughlin."

"Oh! I'm sorry—"

"But everyone has always called me Johnny."

He smiles at me and I smile back.

"Johnny, then."

The men are singing again:

'Twas early in the morning, afore the break of day,
We hoisted British colors and anchored at York's bay.
The sails were bein' lassoed, and hangin' out to dry,
The Irish heroes landing, the Lord knows we must die.

Johnny shakes his head. "A poor choice for a soldiers' song, I think. Colonel Bouquet oughtn't allow it."

"How so?"

"A song about homesickness, and helplessness, and fear of dying in battle? It's bad for morale."

"Surely not. King George has commanded the Irish lads to leave their homes and come here to fight. Our soldiers feel sorry for them, for no one presses anyone into service in these United States."

Johnny looks startled. "How do you know about that?"

"I went to a Quaker school in Philadelphia, and I know of the Lancaster County Amish. The Quakers and the Amish don't believe in warfare. Their fathers and sons are not soldiers."

Johnny looks away. "You've a mind of your own, then. I suppose we have Philadelphia to thank for that."

"W-what do you mean, sir? I—"

Through fields of blood we waded: the cannon's mighty roar,
And many a gallant soldier-lad, lay bleedin' in his gore."

I cover my ears. I can't listen, it's just too sad.

"The song is almost over. Shall I escort you back to the Mess, Miss Zane? May I call you Betsy?"

"Yes. I mean, thank you." My heart begins racing again.

I dance the Foxglove, the Charleston Reel, the Boston Quickstep, and Lost in the Hay with Lieutenant Johnny McGlaughlin. I understand why there is such a thing as dancing. We're together, even if we have nothing to say to each other.

Yet.

The Garden Gate is one of those new dances in a square, and Mr. Stalnaker walks us through the steps before we begin. Eb and Aunt Bessie are in our square. Aunt Bessie, her eyebrows lifting higher and higher, watches me as I smile up at Johnny.

After the Garden Gate we go outside for some fresh air. Johnny insists on fetching my scarf and mittens, my cloak, even though I say I'm not cold.

I almost snap, "I'm as hot as a Philadelphia August. The last thing I need is more clothes." But I stop myself. Instead I say, "Thank you, good sir," in a soft voice.

He bows and goes inside for my wraps.

Betsy, what on earth was that all about?

Back in Philadelphia my friend Sarah Peabody could ride with the best of them, jumping four-foot fences as though they were footstools. But put a young man in front of her, and she would turn into a blushing, helpless damsel, unable to get up from a chair by herself.

Why pretend to be meek and fragile? Surely her beaux could see right through her?

I hear a man's voice from the treeline. "Betsy."

"Mr. McGlaughlin, I'm not cold. I don't need my wraps. Really, I'm quite comfortable."

He stands within the shadows and doesn't say anything. I can just make out the glints of hatchets and knife blades, and the outline of buckskinned shoulders.

"Lewis Wetzel? Is that you?" I say.

Go away! Go away! Please don't spoil the ball.

"McGlaughlin . . . that would be Lieutenant McGlaughlin," Lewis says in a sad voice. "I heard the party. I thought I might see you here."

"I can only stay a moment. Lewis, you can't spend your life hiding in the forest. Come back to Fort Henry at daybreak. They need you. Face the music."

"Face a firing squad, most likely."

"They won't shoot you—your aim's too good."

Lewis laughs. "You say what you think, Betsy. I've always admired that about you."

"Or go back to Pittsburgh and work as a river pilot."

"Too many soldiers at Fort Pitt and Pittsburgh now, Betsy, what with the War headin' west."

"Oh. I hadn't thought of that."

"You're wearing your Christmas dress."

"Lewis Wetzel, how do you know I wore this dress at Christmas?"

I hear a gasp from the shadows. Then: "It's Christmas red, ain't it?"

"It was you! On Christmas Day Eb found footsteps in the snow on the river porch. We were afraid it was Shawnee, but it was you. Lewis, what kind of Christmas is that?"

"Better'n most," he mumbles.

"Betsy," Johnny calls out. He walks toward me, my cloak hanging over his arm. He's holding two punch cups.

"Johnny, this is Lewis Wetzel—"

"Where? Where?"

"Right here." But of course Lewis is long gone.

"Colonel Bouquet would like a word with him," Johnny says grimly, handing me a cup half full of maple syrup. I scoop snow into my cup and stir the melting snow and syrup with my fingers.

"That's what I told him, that he should enlist at Fort Henry. The army needs him."

"Betsy, he tomahawked two old men in cold blood," Johnny says in a low voice. "Neutral Delaware. The Colonel wants him in the stockade before he does anything worse."

"I don't remember a time when I didn't know Lewis Wetzel," I reply. "Even as a boy, he . . . I don't know . . . walked in darkness? Being a captive just made it worse, I suppose. If he enlisted, perchance Colonel Bouquet would look the other way?

"Johnny, he spent Christmas Day spying on us. Can you imagine anything more pitiful?"

"Don't you worry your pretty little head about Lewis Wetzel. We'll take care of him."

"Of course I'm going to worry about Lewis. He's been a good friend to the Zanes all my life."

"Of course," Johnny says coldly. "Good night, Miss Zane."

He leaves me standing there in the moonlight.

———————————

Later that night Aunt Bessie sits on my bed, candle in hand. "Out with it, Betsy. Five dances in a row with the same handsome young man? All of Fort Henry is talking."

"His name is Lieutenant John McGlaughlin. He asked me to call him Johnny."

She leans forward. "A lieutenant? Already? He can't be more than sixteen."

"I thought we were getting along fine, but I must have said something wrong."

Briefly, I tell her about Lewis Wetzel.

Aunt Bessie smiles. "And the lieutenant told you not to worry your pretty head about him?"

"That is what he said. I told him I will worry about Lewis. He's a good friend."

Aunt Bessie smiles and shakes her head. "Oh, Betsy."

"What did I say that was so wrong?"

She thinks for a moment before answering.

"Men want their women to be delicate, retiring creatures."

"I walked from Philadelphia to Pittsburgh! I'm not a delicate, retiring creature."

"I didn't say you had to be delicate and retiring, just that men like to think it so."

"I don't understand, Aunt Bessie."

"Men think it's their job to protect us. If you're shy and delicate, that makes the task all the easier. They won't have to worry about one of their women galloping madly down a river trail on a spirited horse with Indian sign all around."

"You're talking about Eb," I say softly. "At first he didn't want me to ride. Now he chastises me because I don't ride aside on a sidesaddle. I'd break my neck, galloping the river trail in a lady's saddle."

Aunt Bessie takes my hand. "You are your own best comfort, Betsy. That means be yourself, especially on a galloping horse. The trick is, show your Johnny just a little bit of your true nature at a time. He'll come around." She squeezes my hand. "Eb did."

She kisses me good night and walks downstairs.

Comfort, I think, yawning hugely. What was it somebody else told me about comfort, or the like? Something about me being the only one who can take care of myself, because I'm the only one who knows what I want from life?

I'm too sleepy to remember.

10

The War

Eb does not approve of Johnny. When Johnny comes calling this Easter Sunday, Eb blocks the doorway and won't even let him into the house. I have to talk to him at the gate as though I were a hired girl.

"My brother doesn't much care for soldiers," I try to explain. "I'm sorry. He's always been this pigheaded."

"But I'm an officer in the Continental Army, just like Colonel Zane," Johnny replies.

Eb doesn't want me to marry into the army, I want to say, but of course I don't.

I turn toward Zane House and see Aunt Bessie looking at us through the front window. Her eyebrows are even higher than they were last night.

As I turn toward Johnny, he looks away. There's a bit of a blush across his face, like a ripening peach. He taps the fence post lightly with his boot.

"I've watched you riding your mare, Betsy," he says.

"The Merry May is wonderful."

"I have an Arabian gelding named Pasha. Perhaps we could go for a ride someday," he says shyly, "and have a meal together in a nearby glade."

"I'd like that very much, Johnny."

Now every window has a face in it. Aunt Bessie and her children peer through the front windows. Silas, Andrew, and Jonathan watch me from their second-story window. Even Eb is watching, arms folded in front of him, glaring at me from the sitting-room window. I want to die, I'm so embarrassed.

"I apologize for my family." I gesture toward the windows. "I'll ask Aunt Bessie to invite you to supper this week. We *are* Virginians; my brothers will have to behave like gentlemen."

"Betsy," he says uncomfortably, "I've come to apologize to you. I shouldn't have left you alone last night, not with that scoundrel Lewis Wetzel lurking about. That was behavior unbefitting a gentleman. I'm sorry."

"No, it is I who am sorry. Lewis—"

"If he's . . . a friend, I shouldn't presume. I do apologize."

"Lewis is just a friend of the family."

He gives me his smile and that little tilt of the head again.

I turn my back on the Zanes. "Johnny, tell me about your home. Leave nothing out."

Standing ankle deep in wet snow, and despite a breeze gone from light to brisk, my new beau talks fondly of Tidewater Virginia. He speaks to me of the slow pace of plantation life, where the time of day is reckoned by the meals; of a big white house with a wide porch facing the Potomac River; of peacocks on the lawn; of cotton, indigo, and tobacco fields as far as the eye can see.

He and his mother are avid foxhunters and ride to hounds with the sixth Lord Fairfax's White Post Hunt. The McGlaughlins have, on occasion, ridden to hounds with none other than General George Washington himself, who started his own pack with offspring from Lord Fairfax's imported foxhounds.

I say politely, "It all sounds so grand. Not at all like a tiny pioneer outpost on the Ohio."

"Zane Station won't stay tiny for long," he replies. "Despite our nation's youth, the Tidewater is already old and her people set in their ways. I envy you your chance to live in a corner of Virginia that is still so fresh and new."

"You mean to stay here, then?" I ask, holding my breath. "After this war, and your officer's commission, are over?"

"My older brother will inherit the plantation."

I steal a glance at him just as he steals a glance at me.

Tonight while lying in bed, I hear Aunt Bessie downstairs murmuring seamlessly, like the constant buzz of a beehive. Her voice is pitched too low for me to hear the words.

Every once in a while I hear Eb shout, "Never!" or "I am *not* being impossible!" but with less and less conviction in his voice.

Finally, I hear the front door slam. I rush to the window and, in the starlight, watch Eb stomp his way to the stable.

I go to sleep smiling, knowing that I'll have a good

130

excuse to see Johnny tomorrow. I'm going to invite him to Thursday's supper.

———————

I had forgotten how quickly, and with what vigor, spring comes to the Ohio Valley. The forest pools break their icy fetters as the warm winds swell the grain. It is only the third of April, and already the dogwoods are in bloom— their lovely white arms a stark contrast to the mountain pines. The wild cherries have turned creamy pink. The bloodroot and trillium cover the forest floor with flowers so white, they look like fresh snow. Violets turn the pastures and newground a brilliant bluish-purple.

Carolina parakeets, bluebirds, orioles, yellow finches, and scarlet tanagers decorate the leafed-out trees with their bright feathers. The air is scented with wildflowers and filled with bird song. After only one week in the earth, Aunt Bessie's rosebush has taken hold. Tiny leaves, and buds the size of a baby's milk teeth, cover the branches.

On Thursday Johnny knocks on the door just after sunset.

He steps into Zane House smelling of soap and carrying two sprigs of dogwood blossom. He gives one sprig to Aunt Bessie and the second to me. After thanking him, I place both in a pewter tankard. I fill it with water before setting it on our table as a centerpiece.

We partake of fried catfish, pickles, potatoes, and venison. Rachel baked cornbread just this morning. I bring out the last jar of Old Bess's blackberry jam.

While the rest of us make small talk, Eb spends the entire meal glaring at Lieutenant McGlaughlin.

After dinner we sit before the fire, drinking pre-War coffee with real sugar as a treat. Eb sets his cup down with a bang.

"Lieutenant, has my little sister told you my opinion of soldiers?" Eb demands.

"She has, Colonel Zane. And yet, where would our nation be today without her army?" Johnny asks in a mild voice.

"This is wartime, true enough," Eb replies. "But in peace or not, no sister of mine is going to be a camp follower, married or not. What are your intentions after this war is over?"

My face burns as hot as the hearth fire.

"I'm quite partial to the wilderness, Colonel. Surely, Zane Station will become a proper town after the war. I understand the Delaware name for our island is Wheeling. That would be a fine name for a new settlement. Or perhaps Zanestown or Zanesville. Colonel Bouquet tells me the Zanes were the very first settlers here, way back in 1769. A new, bustling town, at the very gateway into this beautiful country, should be named after the Zanes. Don't you agree?"

Eb smiles under his beard. "You Tidewater Virginians are polite, I'll give you that. You intend to live on the frontier?"

"Sir, all I want is at Zane Station," Johnny says in a firm voice. He looks into my eyes. "I've studied law and surveying. I can earn a living as a private citizen of these United States."

———————————

My mornings are spent teaching the Zane and Bouquet small fry in our "schoolhouse," the southeast corner of the ground floor. Elizabeth, Sarah, and Yvonne can read haltingly the Mother Goose rhymes I write on our gray slate. Stephen, and now Noah as well, practice writing letters and numbers on that same slab.

My afternoons are spent riding—Johnny on Pasha, and myself on the Merry May.

Johnny doesn't like to ride very far from Fort Henry. "The savages are all around us, Betsy," he tells me.

"What nonsense," I say in a scornful voice. "I've been riding the river trail since October. I've never seen an Indian."

I've learned to ride ahead of him so he has no choice but to go where I lead.

This afternoon we bring a simple meal in our saddlebags—cornbread, smoked venison, and dried apple slices—and find a glade filled with clover. As we sit down, our legs crush the blossoms. I breathe in their honey scent. Pasha and the Merry May dip their heads and crop the new grass.

I can't remember a time when I felt so dizzy with happiness, so complete, and yet, like a rosebud, so full of promise and possibilities. And all because of the young man sitting next to me.

"An apple slice, Betsy?"

"Thank you. You really meant it, what you said last week? You mean to stay here after the War?"

"Every word. . . . Betsy?"

"Yes?"

His lips catch mine—thank goodness, before I put a chunk of apple in my mouth. But I'm so surprised, I forget to notice what my first kiss feels like. Too soon it's over.

Johnny says. "You shouldn't be seated astride. Ladies should sit aside, and on a lady's saddle. You're a lady, Betsy. You're my lady, and you should be seated as one."

"I've no doubt seated aside in a black velvet riding habit from Paris is proper for the White Post Hunt. But this is the wilderness."

"Surely a Philadelphia lady knows how to ride as one?"

"I do," I say slowly, trying not to let the anger creep into my voice. "I have not used a sidesaddle since I was ten. It's too dangerous for the sort of riding I like."

"To be seated like a man is unladylike, unseemly—"

"Johnny, I used to ride along the Schuylkill River with school friends. We always rode cross saddle, in knitted-silk *pantalons,* which are all the rage among Parisian horse-women, by the way. We were proper Philadelphia ladies, all of us."

"You won't do this for my happiness?" he asks angrily.

"Your happiness, at the expense of mine?" I snap back. "You've taken one kiss from me, Lieutenant, and now you're telling me how to ride my horse?"

Quickly, he rises to his feet.

"Johnny, please, don't be cross with me, not on such a

134

beautiful spring day," I implore him. "Come, I want to show you where I found my brother Isaac last October."

Feeling a bit foolish, I allow him to help me to my feet. We pack up the remains of our meal and ride hard, weaving along the river trail. By now I know this trail like the back of my hand. I know just where to dodge the branches, just when to sit deep in the saddle with my feet outstretched in the stirrups as we cross gulleys and washes. We dismount at the bottom of the hill.

"Right there," I say, pointing to a wide patch on the sandbar. "Isaac was clutching a log as though his life depended on it. Which I suppose it did, come to think of it."

"Would you like a drink from my canteen, Betsy?" Johnny asks. He turns to his saddlebag. Pasha's nostrils flare, and he tries to back up. "Easy, Pasha, easy, boy."

The Merry May is restless too. Her hooves prance on the slippery riverbank. "What is it, May?" I ask as she stares, wide-eyed, at a stout tree trunk.

I see a little boy with a broad forehead, and dark hair and eyes, peeping at May and Pasha from behind the tree. Buckskins I'm used to, but his two long braids freeze my blood. Another boy, smaller than the first, is watching the horses, too.

I hear the *click* of metal against metal. Johnny has cocked his pistol.

"Johnny, no! They're children."

Of course they've disappeared. I hear them tearing downstream and through the woods.

Johnny turns to me, his pupils pinpoints of fury.

"I told you we shouldn't have ridden this far from the fort," he says in a low, angry voice. "Mount and ride."

"But—"

"That's an order!"

I have my left foot in the stirrup when a voice cries out.

"Hear me! I'm Isaac Zane of Zane Station, Virginia. I mean you no harm."

"Isaac?" I call out. "It's Betsy. Where are you?"

Isaac steps from behind another tree and walks toward us, arms outstretched. Just behind him is a young woman. The little boys run to her and clutch at her deerskin skirt. She places her hands on their heads.

I say, "You must be Myeerah." She turns at the sound of her name, but there is no expression in her face. Isaac says something to her in Wyandot. When I hear "Betsy," her eyes widen. She nods to me and gives me a hint of a smile.

"Isaac, this is Lieutnant John McGlaughlin. Johnny, this is my brother, Isaac Zane."

"Pleased to meet you, Lieutenant." Isaac holds out his hand.

Johnny has placed his pistol in his belt, but he watches the little family closely. All of a sudden I see Isaac through his eyes. A white man, to be sure, but dressed as a Wyandot in breechcloth and leggings. Tattoos swirl across his right shoulder and chest. His skull has been plucked clean except for a plume of black hair on top, like the feathered crest of a bird of prey.

I turn to look at Johnny, seeing him now through Isaac's

136

eyes. A soldier, armed, who could kill him, his wife, and his sons and ride back to Fort Henry a hero. My sister-in-law and nephews look at Johnny without a hint of trust in their faces.

Johnny slowly extends his right hand and takes Isaac's. "Mr. Zane," he says stiffly.

"Lieutenant McGlaughlin."

Isaac turns to me. "I need to talk to the family."

———————————

"Have you come back for good, Isaac?" Ebenezer asks coldly.

Spring rain beats against the windowpanes. We are all sitting before the fire. Aunt Bessie, her children hiding behind her, lays out cornbread, bacon, and milk for Isaac's family.

Isaac's boys, hiding behind Myeerah, eye the food and lick their lips.

"Please," Aunt Bessie says, nodding toward the platters. "You must be cold and hungry.

"Elizabeth, Sarah, Noah," she says, pushing her children in front of her, "you needn't be afraid. These boys are your cousins. They're your uncle Isaac's sons."

Isaac says something to Myeerah. She reaches for a chunk of cornbread, breaks it in two, and hands the pieces to her children. My nephews gobble the cornbread down in two gulps, then eye the bacon. They remind me of those starving, dancing dogs in the High Street Market back in Philadelphia.

I pour milk into two tankards and stir some molasses

into each. The boys gulp hard from the tankards and set them, empty, on the table. With mouths full of bacon, they speak in shy voices.

Isaac says, "White Hawk and White Owl say, 'Thank you, our father's sisters.'"

"They look like you, Isaac," I say, pouring out more milk for them. "I thought they looked familiar, when I saw them hiding behind that tree."

"Have you come back for good, Isaac?" Eb repeats, but in a warmer tone of voice.

Isaac leans forward in his chair. "I've come to warn you, Eb. Warn all of you here at Fort Henry. . . . Is there more food in the kitchen, Bess? Something your little ones would like?"

"Rachel's made some molasses snaps," Aunt Bessie says faintly. She leads her children into the kitchen and returns with cookies for White Hawk and White Owl, closing the door behind her.

"Have you heard what happened to the Delaware missions along the Tuscawaras River?" Isaac asks.

"We've heard nothing," Eb replies.

"Not surprised. I'd like to think they're not proud of it now," Isaac says dryly. "What day is today?"

"April ninth," Jonathan answers.

"Must have been late February. Colonel David Williamson marched a detachment from Fort Pitt. They rounded up the Delaware from Salem and Schoenbrunn and marched them to Gnadenhutten."

Isaac took a deep breath. "A month ago today, then.

Those soldiers murdered ninety-four people. Old men and women. Mothers. Children. Babes-in-arms. They killed them all."

"But the Christian Delaware are neutral," Silas says in a shocked voice.

"Colonel Williamson was not of the same opinion," Isaac replies.

"That's what Lewis Wetzel said on the flatboat coming here," I say, my voice shaking. "He said no one is ever neutral."

Isaac looks at me coldly. "These people were."

"Of course they were, Isaac. Surely you don't think I'd be in agreement with Lewis Wetzel concerning Indians?"

"Not you, Betsy," he says softly.

"How do you know this for a fact, Isaac?" Eb asks gently. "If they were all murdered?"

"Two escaped, a boy named Adam Stroud and a girl named Esther. They ran back to Schoenbrunn to warn those who'd been hiding in the fields. They all ran north to Wingenund's Town. Wingenund's Delaware have never been neutral. They're on the warpath, all of them, along with the Shawnee, Miami, Wyandot, even some Potawatomi and Chippewa from the west. They'll attack Fort Henry."

I sit in stunned silence, unable to take it in.

"Damn them!" Eb shouts, pounding the table. "Williamson and his men have hightailed it back to Fort Pitt, leaving us to pay the price for their cowardice!"

Silas leans forward. "And what of Netawatwees Sachem? And Glickihigan?"

"Who are they?" I ask.

"Adam Stroud said both elders were there. He said Netawatwees Sachem was leading them in the Twenty-third Psalm as a soldier bashed his head in with a rifle butt."

Jonathan covers his face with his hands. "Silas and I met them both when we were captives of the Delaware," he says in a faint voice. "They were old men, even twenty years ago."

We sit in silence for a moment before Isaac turns to Aunt Bessie. "Esther remembered a major with a missing left arm. That sounds like Major McCullough, Bess."

"My brother Samuel would never do such a thing," Aunt Bessie whispers hoarsely. "Esther must have been mistaken."

"I remember Uncle Samuel," I say. "Esther must have seen another one-armed major."

Isaac looks away, toward his children, and says nothing.

"The War is finally coming to Fort Henry," Silas says softly.

In the stalls Aunt Bessie's milk cow, Pansy, gives a deep moo. Maybelle and the Merry May whinny to Pasha, who answers the mares with a snort.

"No more riding, Betsy," Eb and Johnny say together.

Tonight I lie awake and listen as hard rain beats against Zane House. The wind howls like a wolf pack and sets the oiled-paper windowpanes in my bedroom to crackling.

Elizabeth and Sarah lie next to me, snug and well

wrapped within layers of the deepest sleep. The heavy weather does not bestir them.

To me sleep is as far away as the Philadelphia Zane House on Third and Church Streets. I stare hard into the utter blackness, searching for . . . what?

Isaac didn't want Elizabeth, Sarah, and Noah to know about the warpath and its reasons. But if there is a battle, they'll find out soon enough.

Just this morning a company of soldiers left Fort Henry and paddled downstream to defend Fort Washington. Eb complained loud and long to Colonel Bouquet, but it did no good; Fort Henry is near abandoned.

A battle here could mean the death of all of us: the Zanes, the Bouquets, Johnny, and the soldiers who remain.

Maybelle and the Merry May would be taken across the Ohio as war booty. Surely they'd spend the rest of their lives wondering why I wasn't with them.

Silas said the War has finally come to Fort Henry. That means it's the Zanes' turn to prove their mettle. But what can an almost fourteen-year-old girl do?

"I am my own best comfort," I whisper into the darkness.

I do know what I want from life, and I reckon I know what it means to be a lady: I need the freedom to take care of myself, but I'm obliged to care for others as well. Anything less, and I'd be no better off than Lewis Wetzel, wandering as a solitary in the wilderness, jabbering to the blue jays and grasshoppers.

A crack of lightning illuminates the bedroom walls for

a moment. My father built Zane House to be a fortress: double walled with narrow windows. These third-story windows are loopholes, tapered notches into which a rifle barrel can be placed.

The Wyandot Zanes are downstairs, as well-fed, snug, and dry as the rest of us. What would this night have been like for Isaac and his family, out in the raging storm, if they hadn't come home?

The Virginia Zane House seemed so strong and safe this morning. Despite standing stalwart against the weather, these double-oaken walls now seem as flimsy as paper.

11

The Colonels

I write on our slab of gray slate:

Elizabeth, Elspeth, Betsy, and Bess,
They all went together to seek a bird's nest;
They found a bird's nest with five eggs in,
They all took one, and left four in.

"Who can read this? Elizabeth? Sarah? Noah?"

Morning sun streams through the southeast window. My nieces and nephews sit before me, their questioning, terrified gazes fixed on my face. White Owl and White Hawk are as restless and jittery as wild birds locked up in a cage.

Early May is as hot as June, and yet no one is allowed to leave Zane House. We sit before the dampened hearth fire as skittish as rabbits. Every rifle fire or shout from Fort Henry bolts us right out of our seats.

I point to the "a" in Elizabeth. "Everyone knows this *first* letter. White Owl?"

Silence, then Sarah raises her hand.

"Good for you, Sarah! I know you can read this verse."

"Aunt Betsy?" she whispers. "When will the soldiers and Indians be here?"

How can she know about what's coming? It's supposed to be a secret.

I look out the open front door. Aunt Bessie and Rachel Johnson are just outside, boiling dresses and linens in a caldron suspended over a fire. My brothers stand in front of them, each with a rifle primed and ready. The drifting steam stinks of lye soap and sets our eyes to watering.

Myeerah sits by the hearth fire.

"Uncle Isaac and his family are here. The soldiers are at Fort Henry. There's nothing to worry about," I say in a cheerful voice.

Sarah, Noah, White Hawk, and White Owl all look toward Elizabeth, the oldest.

"Sarah means the bad ones," Elizabeth says softly.

I look at the small, frightened faces around me. When I was little, no adult could keep anything from me, no matter how hard he or she tried. Even Isaac, the best secret keeper among the Zanes, couldn't keep this one from Elizabeth, Sarah, and Noah. White Hawk and White Owl must know about the impending battle, too.

"I don't know when the bad ones are coming," I say quickly. "No one knows. We'll have no more school today, but stay inside. Noah, play pirates with your cousins. Girls, work on your samplers. Great-Aunt Elizabeth used to say a lady who can't use a needle is as scandalous as a man who can't use a sword."

Talking of swords was a mistake. Elizabeth, Sarah, and

144

Noah commence to cry. White Hawk and White Owl run to their mother.

In the wink of an eye Isaac puts his rifle down, comes inside, and sits on the floor next to us. "I'll tell you another family story," he declares, "but you have to be quiet." Elizabeth, Sarah, and Noah settle down soon enough.

"Thank you, Isaac," I say softly.

Isaac has been telling us pioneer stories about our parents and grandparents. Our father, Nathaniel Zane, and our grandfather, another Ebenezer Zane, fought off bears and wolves, tornadoes and floods, French trappers and hostile Indians, so we could sit here in the Virginia Zane House and listen to stories about their exploits. The stories bolster my courage and resolve and are almost exciting enough to make me forget about the warpath.

My clothes are sticking to me, my hair is sweaty ropes on my neck; I'd give just about anything for a swim. I remember frolicking with Maybelle and the Merry May in the Delaware last summer. Even swimming in that filthy river, with the jeers of randy sailors in my ears, was better than being cooped up all day and fearing the worst.

Maybelle and the Merry May stand day after sultry day, shut up in the stable. Every once in a while they give their stall walls a doleful kick. It must be torture for them, to smell the tender spring grass growing in their new paddock and not be able to get to it. Every morning one of my brothers arms himself to the teeth, slips out the back door, and runs to the stables to grain and water the horses and Aunt Bessie's milk cow, Pansy. He comes back with a bucket of warm milk.

This evening, the twenty-third of May, is a steamy, moonless night. I toss back and forth, unable to sleep as the sweat rolls off my forehead and soaks my pillow. My horses aren't sleeping, either. I hear them snort, nicker, and scrape at the stall floors in boredom and frustration. I know just how they feel.

I get up, steal down the stairs, and lift the latch on the back door. Silently I climb over the paddock fence. The pasture grass smells spicy sweet as I tear handfuls out of the ground. I open the stable door, feel my way to the stalls, and hold out the fodder to their noses.

"Maybelle, the Merry May, it's me," I whisper softly.

I can't see them in the utter blackness, but I feel their hot breath on my face. Their lips brush against my palms. I hear their munching and snorts of pleasure.

"Good girls," I whisper. "It's hard, I know, bolted up like prisoners. But you're luckier than the rest of us, because you don't know why you can't go outside."

I wrap my arms around Maybelle's neck. "I'm so scared," I whisper into her warm coat. "We all expect an attack. Any breath might be my last."

The acrid scents of gunpowder and tobacco drift across the stable. Someone else is here, someone with a musket.

A deep voice says, *"Nekahnoh, ah quoi teti?"*

Indians in the stable! My knees collapse under me; I fall to the floor.

"Please don't shoot me, sir," I beg the darkness. "I mean no harm."

"Betsy?"

My brother Silas pulls me up roughly by my arm.

"What are you doing out here?" he whispers angrily.

"My horses yearn for spring grass. They don't understand why they can't get to it."

"I could have killed you! Shot you dead!"

I lean against him and start to cry. "Silas, I'm so scared," I sob. "Waiting for the worst. I can't sleep."

"Shh . . . Betsy, shh." He rubs my head hard, as though he were stroking a horse's neck. "Inside with you. I won't tell Eb."

I wipe my eyes and sniff. "As long as we're out here, could you help me give them more fodder?"

Silas chuckles softly. "Shawnee all around us and my little sister wants to hand feed her horses as though they were lapdogs."

He helps me pull the tender shoots out of the ground. We fill two buckets with grass. As a false dawn lights the sky, I see the smudged outlines of a gray treeline and a gray stable. And as the false dawn turns true, I see that Silas is dressed in deerskin leggings and a breechcloth. With his long black hair he looks like an Indian.

"What did you say to me? That wasn't English."

"It was Shawnee. When Jonathan and I were Delaware captives, we got to know their neighbors the Shawnee as well. I called you a friend and remarked on the heat."

"Do you think they'll attack? Do you really think so?"

Silas says slowly, "I've never met a more trusting, open-hearted people than those Christian Delaware, or a prouder people than the Shawnee. Our army has betrayed the Delaware and shown the Shawnee how vulnerable they are. The Wyandot and the Miami would rather fight us now than later. Every brave in the Ohio country is on the warpath, Betsy.

"The tribes have been armed by the British, but first and foremost they're fighting for themselves. They don't want any of us—British, French, or American—west of the Ohio River. Isaac is right to spare the small fry, but you're old enough to know how bad it really is."

We walk into the stable with our buckets of grass. "Do you guard the livestock every night? When do you sleep, Silas?"

"We take turns, the five of us. But Jonathan will be leaving this morning, as a scout for Colonel Crawford and Colonel Williamson. Five hundred men should be here from Fort Pitt. Jonathan's going to lead the army across the Ohio and northwest to the Big and Little Sandusky Rivers. They're going to attack the Delaware, Wyandot, and Shawnee towns up there."

"Before *they* attack *us,* you mean." I set the buckets down on the stall floors. As Maybelle and the Merry May commence to eat, Pansy moos at me pleadingly. She wants fresh fodder, too.

"That is the army's intention. You'd best go to bed, Betsy."

"I reckon we're fighting for ourselves, as well," I say. "I'm glad Isaac came home. If he'd stayed in Tarhe's Town, our army might have killed him and our nephews. What about Pansy?"

"I reckon Isaac was thinking of just that. I'll fetch another bucket of fodder for Pansy."

"The small fry figured it out, about the warpath, Silas."

I hear him cursing under his breath. "They're no longer small fry then, I reckon. Go to sleep, Betsy."

Late morning the soldiers arrive in flatboats from Fort Pitt. They look more like farmers than fighting men. They stand in little groups scratching, smoking, and gazing at the sky as though to assess the weather for their crops back home.

Their packhorses just about break my heart, bony ribbed and scabby skinned, with bellies swollen from worms and starvation. Their flanks are already foamy with sweat just from walking up the hill. Each horse stands in a cloud of flies.

Colonel Crawford and Colonel Williamson come into the house to collect Jonathan. Aunt Bessie gives them burnt-cornhusk coffee. Colonel William Crawford has a big belly just like *Jule Nisse*, or Sint Nicholaas. White hair and a long white beard completely frame his face. He holds his sides and laughs merrily at Noah, who's holding a stick across his shoulder like a rifle and marching back and forth.

A smiling Colonel David Williamson watches Noah from a bench near the wall. He looks so ordinary: ordinary brown hair, ordinary straight nose. No Devil's horns sprout from his temples, no demon's hooves clatter on the floor. I

149

study his hands, the very hands that crushed infant heads with his rifle butt. Now they are holding a pretty china cup. I glance at his rifle, but all I see is gleaming metal and a shiny bird's-eye maple stock.

He's scrubbed it clean. Or ordered someone to.

"Jonathan's been watching the river all morning," I say. "I'll fetch him."

Jonathan is standing on the river porch, gazing at the Ohio. I have to call his name out twice before he answers.

"I heard you the first time, Betsy," he says softly.

"Colonel Williamson is here," I say. "How can you work for that monster?"

Jonathan turns to me with a start. "Listen to me, Betsy," he whispers fiercely, holding my arm fast. "I'm not working for Colonel Williamson. I'm working for the Zanes. Understand?"

"No." I wrest my arm away.

"The more Indians the Zanes can keep on the Ohio side of the river, the better."

"I understand," I say rubbing my arm. "But Jonathan, Colonel Williamson looks so ordinary. Could Isaac have been wrong about the massacre?"

"Isaac wasn't wrong," Jonathan says in a hollow voice. "Betsy, it's meant a lot to me, your coming home. I've missed you."

A shadow crosses my heart. "You sound as if you're saying farewell. You will come back, won't you, Jonathan?"

"That is my intention. Just now I need a bit more time alone, sister. The French *voyageurs* call the Ohio *la belle rivière*,

150

the beautiful river. I need to watch the beautiful river, just a bit more."

———————————

The Zanes and the colonels share a meal of squirrel stew, cornbread, salted catfish, greens from the kitchen garden, and the last of the rose-hip tea sweetened with the last of my Lady's Day honey. The colonels eat quickly and at length. No one speaks.

Finally, Colonel Crawford pushes himself away from the table. "A fine meal, Mrs. Zane," he says. "A fine meal in good company. Thank you very much. Scout, are you ready?"

Jonathan nods and reaches for his raccoon cap.

Colonel Williamson stands up. "Mrs. Zane? Ever since I've crossed your threshold, you've looked at me as though you had a question. Am I right?"

Aunt Bessie takes a deep breath. "I was a McCullough before I married Ebenezer Zane, Colonel Williamson. What do you hear of my brother, Major Samuel McCullough?"

"Sam's your brother? He's a brave man, Mrs. Zane; you can be proud of Sam McCullough. He was with me on the Gnadenhutten Campaign," Colonel Williamson replies.

"No," she whispers.

"Sam's all right, Mrs. Zane. You needn't worry," Colonel Williamson says agreeably. "He's been given extended leave with your brother John. I believe they intend to do some catfishing."

We stand and wait for Aunt Bessie to open the door to bid our guests good-bye. Instead she sits alone at the table, lost in her own thoughts. Eb clears his throat and catches my eye. I open the door for the colonels.

"My sister-in-law is worried about her children," I say by way of apology. "Thank you so much for calling on us."

"Miss Zane," Colonel Crawford says, "you and your family are the very reason we are fighting this war. That we may all be free."

He bows to me and kisses my hand. Colonel Williamson does the same, and it's all I can do not to pull away from him.

Eb and I watch from our dock as all five hundred men, twenty horses, ten officers, Jonathan, and two other scouts, named John Slover and Thomas Nicholson, cross the Ohio. Within moments the army disappears into a wilderness as solid as a barricade.

I find Aunt Bessie lying on her bed, a wet handkerchief pressed to her forehead.

"Aunt Bessie? They're gone."

"When I was six," she whispers, "and Samuel was four, he gave me a fistful of wildflowers on May Day. They were crushed and almost steaming, they were so hot. But he wanted to give his big sister a present. I'll never forget the look on his face as he slowly unfolded his hand."

She rolls over onto her stomach.

"Samuel, how could you?" she wails into the pillow. "Oh, Sam."

"They must have been mistaken, Aunt Bessie. Uncle

Samuel would never kill children, not with nieces and nephews of his own."

She buries her head in her pillow and sobs.

I stand outside on the river porch on the very same spot where Jonathan stood just this morning. I watch the same riverbank, the same currents dividing the Ohio as they flow around Wheeling Island. My brothers are at the fort; Aunt Bessie is upstairs. There is no one to scold me for sitting outside. I can stay on the river porch for as long as I like.

I think about the last time I saw Samuel McCullough. I was six, the same age as Aunt Bessie when he gave her the wildflowers. Uncle Samuel and I used to race, me running as fast as I could go, Uncle Samuel taking giant strides on his long legs. If I beat him, or if he beat me, his reaction always would be the same. He'd toss his head back and laugh.

He looks ordinary, too. No one could look at Uncle Samuel and think, "There's someone who could kill infants. You can see the evil in him, just as clearly as the nose on his face."

Does that mean evil is ordinary, too? How can we know there's evil in someone, if we can't tell by looking?

If you were in the army and Colonel Williamson ordered you to kill infants, what would you have done, Betsy?

Of course, I'm grateful for General Washington's Continental Army and for the freedom their sacrifices will bring us. But I know, in my heart of hearts, that I could never fight in an army. I could never kill anyone.

Tonight Johnny sneaks out of the west sally port. We meet at the front door, and I lead him around to the river porch.

"Betsy, it's good to see you," he murmurs in my ear. He kisses me again and again.

"Johnny," I say, gently pushing him away, "if you had been at Fort Pitt and were ordered to join the Gnadenhutten Campaign, what might have happened if you'd refused?"

"Refusing an order is a serious offense. The punishment depends on the order refused. It could mean the stocks, or a flogging, the stockade, even a firing squad."

"So Uncle Samuel could have faced a firing squad?"

"Who?" He kisses me again.

"Aunt Bessie's brother was at Gnadenhutten."

Johnny stands back in surprise. "He was?"

"He went to Gnadenhutten to avoid punishment, then?"

Johnny shakes his head. "Colonel Williamson told us that the Gnadenhutten Campaign was a volunteer regiment. Anyone who didn't want to go could refuse, with no penalty to his person or his honor. Those who did volunteer knew . . . what they were going to do."

"Are you saying he wanted to go?" I ask faintly. "Johnny, would you have volunteered?"

I hold my breath, waiting for his answer.

"Never," Johnny says firmly. "There's no honor in killing children."

"Don't tell Aunt Bessie it was a volunteer regiment."

"I expect she already knows, Betsy. Your brother Eb does."

More and more settlers from up and down the river come here for safety. Eb invites the Van Swearingens to stay at our house, but Mr. and Mrs. Van Swearingen join their son Charlie at Fort Henry. Their daughter, thirteen-year-old Lucille, stays with us.

"What of the Shawnee, Miss Van Swearingen?" Eb asks her the first evening at dinner.

Lucille bangs her spoon on her plate. "Everyone always asks us about the Shawnee because of Marmaduke. How can we possibly know what they're thinking? My brother left our family to join them twelve years ago this June."

Eb shrugs his shoulders. "I would have thought, Miss Van Swearingen, that blood is thicker than water."

"Not with 'Duke, it isn't. He was hunting with Charlie when they came across a Shawnee hunting party. 'Duke told his own brother he was leaving us to become a Shawnee.

"I don't remember my brother, Mr. Zane. The Shawnee named him after the blue jacket he was wearing. That's all I know."

Silas says, "Our brother Isaac sees him from time to time. 'Duke lives northwest of here, up the Mad River. Blue Jacket: Wehyahpihehrsehnwah. He's a Shawnee war chief now, foster brother to Tecumseh. He captured Daniel Boone once, but Boone escaped."

"A war chief!" I exclaim. "He's turned completely Shawnee?"

Lucille gives me a look that could freeze July. "Mr. Zane," she says, turning toward Silas, "you and your brothers were captives of the Delaware. After your parents went to Fort Detroit to ransom you home, you stayed home. Why?"

"Everyone who's ever been a captive makes his choice, Miss Van Swearingen. There's no telling who will leave or who will stay."

"You mentioned Isaac. He's elected to stay here?" Lucille asks.

"No, I don't think he has," Silas says slowly. "His spirit is among the Wyandot in Tarhe's Town, next to Blue Jacket's Town, on the Mad River. He's at Zane Station now, but as soon as this battle is over, if there is one, he'll take his family home."

Lucille says bitterly, "Don't tell my parents that 'Duke's become a Shawnee war chief. It would only upset them."

I look closely at Silas, Andrew, and Eb. They all have a faraway look to their gaze. Are they remembering their childhoods among the Delaware? Those same Delaware could attack us at any moment. My brothers will, to a man, fight back just as fiercely as they're able.

My brothers could have made the same choice as Marmaduke Van Swearingen, but they did not. Something made them stay home, something 'Duke didn't have.

"Blue Jacket will come back someday, Lucille," I say. "He's your brother, after all."

Lucille shakes her head and stares at her plate.

12

Vengeance

Almost three weeks later, on June fourteenth, we see two white men in a canoe crossing the Ohio. Eb and Silas run down to the dock and help Jonathan and his fellow scout John Slover hobble up the hill. John Slover is bleeding from the right leg. Soldiers come out of the fort and carry him inside.

We help Jonathan over our threshold. My thirty-three-year-old brother looks to have aged twenty years since I saw him last. Stooped over, he eases himself slowly into a chair by the fire with a deep groan. His face sags, the skin drooping in turkey wattles along his jaw line. His black hair is streaked with gray, but maybe that's from grime and gunsmoke.

He looks at us, then the furniture, and finally Great-Great-Grandfather Karl Zane's portrait, with eyes full of wonder.

"There there were times when I thought I'd never see the Zanes again," he says softly. "Then were times when I was sure of it."

"Tell us of the campaign, Jonathan," Eb says, leaning forward in his chair.

"Eb, give him a chance to catch his breath," I say. "He's half starved and worn to a frazzle."

Jonathan holds up his hand. "Betsy, might there be any more of my applejack, cold in the root cellar?"

"I'll fetch some." I open the door in the hall floor and climb down the ladder into the root cellar. I feel around for a jug, then return to the hearth fire.

Jonathan quaffs deeply at his applejack.

"The thought of this jug kept me going, one foot in front of the other, for days and days," he says in a weary voice. "Cold applejack—sweet as May but with a kick like a mule."

He lifts the jug to his lips again.

"Don't drink too much, brother," Eb says. "Colonel Bouquet will want a full report as soon as possible."

"It was a rout," Jonathan says bitterly. "Five hundred men, most no older than your Johnny, Betsy. Only forty made it back to Fort Pitt. They kept coming at us—Delaware, Shawnee, Wyandot, Miami, Chippewa, Potawatomi, Ottawa, Fox, Sac—there were nations I didn't recognize. I saw warriors on Spanish ponies.

"Blue Jacket, Pimoacan, Twisted Vines, Isaac's father-in-law, Tarhe, Black Snake, Michikiniqua, Wingenund, Monakaduto—I saw all their sachems, leading great armies of warriors. We fought them in the flatlands, grass higher than our heads in places, and retreated within tall stands of trees like islands in a sea of grass."

"The officers?" Aunt Bessie asks.

"Colonel Williamson made it back," Jonathan replies.

"I'm sure he's writing dispatches to General Washington right now, trying to put himself and his blighted career in the best possible light."

"Colonel Crawford?" I ask.

"The Delaware caught Colonel Crawford and Dr. John Knight, took them both back to Wingenund's Town. Dr. Knight escaped and ran south by southeast just as John Slover and I did. By some miracle our paths crossed on the Tuscawaras River. Dr. Knight ought to be back in Fort Pitt by now."

He takes another long pull on the jug.

"You haven't said what happened to Colonel Crawford."

"Betsy, you don't want to hear this."

Silas says, "She's old enough."

Jonathan says softly, "The Delaware tortured him, then burned him to death. Dr. Knight said it took days and days for Colonel Crawford to die. Finally, they let Adam Stroud, that boy who survived Gnadenhutten, scalp him. Dr. Knight wasn't sure if Crawford was alive or not at the time."

That jolly old man tortured to death. And Colonel Williamson safe at Fort Pitt!

"Nothing makes sense anymore," I whisper.

Jonathan gets up slowly.

"In need of doctoring, are you?" Aunt Bessie asks.

"All the doctoring I need is on the river porch, Bess. If someone could help me with a chair."

I drag a chair to his favorite spot. Eb helps Jonathan out the back door. My brother sits down with a deep sigh.

159

A smile creeps over his face as he looks down the cliff at the Ohio River.

"You are so beautiful," he whispers.

"I'll fetch the applejack," I say.

But when I return to the river porch with the jug, Jonathan is fast asleep.

The first week of August, Silas returns from Fort Pitt with more news of what folks are calling the Battle of Sandusky or the Crawford Campaign.

"The fools," he says bitterly. "The colonels thought they had the element of surprise on their side. An army five hundred men strong with a color guard and a fife and drum corps marching through the forests—a surprise? They were spied upon from the moment they left the Ohio Valley.

"Once the army was out of the trees and onto the Sandusky Plains, they were surrounded. Jonathan was right. It was a rout."

Silas turns to Aunt Bessie.

"There's something else, Bess. I saw your brother John at Fort Pitt. He says Samuel was killed on July thirtieth."

The blood drains from Aunt Bessie's face. "Sam?"

"John says they were catfishing, on the Ohio side. They heard gunfire and jumped on their horses. Samuel couldn't gallop, with only one arm. They shot him clean off his horse. John was sure Sam was dead before he hit the ground. It was Delaware, all right."

"How do you know it was Delaware?"

"I just know, Bessie. You don't want to know how I know."

"He was my brother, Silas. I will ask you again."

Silas turns to me. "I'd like some water, Betsy."

"Rachel," I call out. "Silas wants water."

"No," Silas says. "I want you to fetch it."

"But then I can't hear what happened."

"Betsy—"

"Silas, you said I'm old enough to know."

He looks at me with sad, tired eyes. "No one's old enough for this one, Betsy. Go on now."

"But—"

"Do as he says! This instant!" Aunt Bessie shrills at me.

I jump up and run to the kitchen. But I don't shut the door all the way. I peek around it, listening.

"John went back for him once the shooting stopped," Silas says softly. "They'd scalped him, of course. Everyone does that."

"How do you know it was Delaware?" Aunt Bessie asks slowly.

"They'd cut his heart out and taken it with them. I'm really sorry, Bess. The Delaware do that to special enemies. They must have known it was him, without that left arm."

Aunt Bessie drops her head to the table. Her arms curl around her face. Suddenly, she looks up.

"Are you telling me they've eaten his heart? For vengeance?"

Silas looks out the window, toward Fort Henry. "Maybe," he says.

This August reminds me of my last Monday in the High Street Market in Philadelphia. It is fiercely hot and still. All day long sweat runs down my legs and creeps between my toes. My bodice is soaked through by noon. I use enough ribbons and hairpins to forbid even one hair to fall against the back of my neck.

I have long since stopped trying to teach the children. Elizabeth, Sarah, and Noah fight all day and scream their way through nightmares all night. White Hawk and White Owl might as well be Myeerah's shadow, they stick so close to her. In the early morning I've taken to running upstairs and down just to work off the nervous twitches. I'm almost to the point of wanting the battle, just to get it over with.

Colonel Bouquet has forbidden all military personnel to leave Fort Henry. This time he really means it, I reckon, for Johnny hasn't come calling in ages. At sundown he stands in the middle of the parade ground and looks toward Zane House. In my room I peel back the oiled-paper windowpane, reach out my arm, and wave and wave to him.

There is a spring-fed pool just to the west of our apple orchard. The pool feeds a stream that tumbles down the cliffside and into the Ohio. Every dawn I'm able to, I slip out our back door to frolic in the pool, the cold water splashing my shins.

The pool is surrounded by thick brush. No one can see me. This morning I splash and splash until my sweat-stiff dress is soaked through with sparkling-clean water. I lie down in the deepest part of the pool and float on my back. The cold, clean water on my hot, sticky scalp and neck is exquisite. I pitch my head farther back and let the ripples break over my face. I sit up and gulp handfuls of water from the purling spring.

"Yer makin' too much noise, Betsy," a voice calls out.

I bolt out of the water, heart pounding. An instant later I figure out who it is. "I know it's you, Lewis," I call back. "Show yourself."

Lewis Wetzel walks out of a dark patch of trees and into the bright sunlight. I stare at him in shock.

Lewis looks more like a tree than a man. His shredded buckskins are lashed together with vines. His skin is the same mottled gray as a tree trunk. Even his long hair, once as black and glossy as pitch, is the same dull brown of dying leaves.

My shock turns to pity. "Lewis, my brothers believe Fort Henry will be attacked before the first snow. Surely you could give yourself up now. Colonel Bouquet needs you, needs your sure shot."

Instead of answering, Lewis looks at me. His eyes look peculiar—as empty and predatory as a snake's.

"Lewis, did you hear me?"

"Been thinking," he says, "'bout Adam and Eve. How happy they were, just the two of them in the wilderness."

"Adam and Eve?"

He hasn't stopped looking at me with those snake eyes.

His words are slow, his voice thick and sluggish. It occurs to me that he might not have spoken a word since the Saturday-night ball in the Officers' Mess. That was the night before Easter.

"Been thinking," he says again, "'bout happiness."

A shiver of fear runs through me. I am very much aware of my thin muslin dress, soaked through and leaving nothing to the imagination. The wet cloth clings to my legs and pulls at my bodice. I try to lift my skirt away from me. It smacks against my knees and shins. I want to flee.

This is how deer or Indians feel when Lewis is nigh.

I take a step toward home. Lewis takes a step forward.

"Goin' west to the Mississippi. Got it figured. You and me, Betsy. Just like Adam and Eve in our very own wilderness."

"What . . . what do you mean?"

"Been givin' you a lot of thought, these six seasons alone in the wilderness. It's not right, being alone. Adam had Eve."

I whisper, "We're friends, you and I."

My heart is pounding again.

He watches me. "You just turned fourteen, ain't that right, Betsy? I killed five Indians the summer I was fourteen. I've killed thirty more since then, I reckon. Six a year. I track them back to their hunting camps or shoot them right out of their canoes.

"They bring their families with them to the hunting camps so the women can tan the skins. I kill the families, too."

The hair on the back of my neck creeps upward.

"You're the only one who could make me change, Betsy. I'd give up this solitary, murderin' life for you."

"No, I couldn't, Lewis," I stammer. "I can't change who you are."

How could I ever have thought of him as a friend?

He looks bewildered. "A home, Betsy. Adam and Eve."

I point toward the west sally port. "Come back to Fort Henry with me," I say, my voice shaking. "Colonel Bouquet needs you—"

He jumps forward. I give a little scream and jump back.

Lewis's gray face crumples. "Don't be afraid of me," he cries out.

"I'm not afraid of you, Lewis," I say, my voice shrilling in terror, "but I can't leave here. Zane Station is my home."

Lewis opens his arms toward me. "I'm your home, Betsy," he sobs. "You're my home."

"I'm not your home, Lewis."

He falls to his knees, claws at the dirt, and howls.

"Lewis, come back to Fort Henry. You need to be among people again. All this time spent as a solitary . . . surely it's been worse punishment than anything either army could do to you."

Lewis crawls back into the deep shade of the treeline. He crashes through the undergrowth, howling gibberish.

I run home as fast, it seems, as if I were galloping the Merry May down the river trail once again. I push open the front door, enter, slam it shut, and bolt it from the inside.

Home! Safe in Zane House!

Aunt Bessie and Rachel Johnson look up from bread

165

making. "How many times have I told you not to bathe in that spring pool, Betsy," Aunt Bessie scolds. "Your dress is dripping all over the floor, and now the little ones will want to bathe as well."

"Aunt Betsy! Aunt Betsy!" Elizabeth interrupts excitedly. "Come and see what I did! Come and see!"

Elizabeth takes me by the hand and leads me to the southeast corner. The gray slate is leaning against the wall, lit up by the slanting morning sunshine. On it she has written, amid the dips and whorls on the stone:

Elizabeth, Elspeth, Betsy, and Bess,
They all went together to seek a bird's nest;
They found a bird's nest with five eggs in,
They all took one, and left four in.

"I've been writing it," she says shyly, "whenever your back was turned helping Ma with chores. It means we're all 'Elizabeth,' doesn't it?"

"Oh, Elizabeth," I cry out. I gather my niece into my arms and burst into tears.

"Are there mistakes?" she asks. "I've worked so hard."

"It's perfect, perfect." I hold her tighter and sob.

"Betsy," Aunt Bessie says, kneeling beside me. "Is there something wrong? And you're getting Elizabeth's dress all wet."

"I don't mind, Ma. I'm too hot anyway."

I let go of Elizabeth and dry my eyes. "I was just afraid, Aunt Bessie, that's all."

Elizabeth says, "I want to be called Elspeth from now on."

———————————

On August twenty-eighth, in the middle of a steamy afternoon, Major John Linn gallops a near-collapsed horse up the hill to Fort Henry. Old Sam and I are outside, under the stable roof.

"Where's your brother? Where's Colonel Zane?" Major Linn calls to me, his eyes wild in terror.

"Inside," I whisper.

"Take care of my mount," he says to Old Sam. The major near collapses himself jumping down from the saddle.

His mount, a beautiful dappled gray, is trembling all over from exhaustion and dehydration. I want to attend to the horse, but I want even more to hear what Major Linn has to say to Eb. I run inside just as my brother is pulling up a chair for him.

"I was on patrol, on the Ohio side," Major Linn says, panting. I fetch him a tankard of water, and he drinks it dry.

Eb says, "Not too much, Major, you'll founder."

Major Linn takes a deep breath.

"Indians, all in war paint. And British, dressed in green, Queen's Rangers. Maybe six hundred strong. The Indians were on their hands and knees, digging flints out of the ground."

"To make arrowheads," I whisper.

The shock! And terror! More of each than facing the buffalo on the Crofter Road! The War is finally coming to Fort Henry.

Eb says quickly, "We have ten soldiers in the militia. Then there's Colonel Bouquet, Lieutenant McGlaughlin, and another eight settlers. Jonathan, Silas, Andrew, Isaac, myself. There's Old Sam. Plus nine wives, seven children, Bess, Rachel Johnson, and Betsy. The rest are downriver at Fort Washington."

"Eb, Aunt Bessie's not here," I exclaim in horror. "She left for Fort Washington this morning. Her father's ailing."

"I'd forgotten, Bess is gone." I see a look on Eb's face I've not seen there before. *Fear.*

"Forty-four defenders, then," Major Linn says hurriedly, "and myself makes forty-five." He stands up. "Colonel, I'll remount and gallop downriver to Fort Washington and inform Colonel Williamson. He's in command there now."

"Fort Washington is miles away. You and your mount are too tired, Major, but we'll send someone," Eb says. He turns to me. "Betsy, you and Myeerah must gather the children and take them to Fort Henry. Lock them in the central storage."

"But there're no windows in the central storage," I say. "It's pitch-black in there."

"That's right, no windows. Now move!"

I dash up the stairs two at once, then run round the bedrooms, grabbing girls' dresses and extra breeches and shirts for Noah. Downstairs in the kitchen I wrap a cornpone in a napkin and tuck a stoppered water jug under my arm. I tie them both into my apron.

Myeerah is standing next to the hearth, watching me in alarm.

"Myeerah, help me!"

Puzzled, she shakes her head.

"Shawnee," I try to explain. "British! British!"

She gasps just as the fort's bell rings out a warning.

"What are you doing?" Eb shouts at me. "Get to the fort now!"

I grasp Aunt Bessie's children by their wrists. White Hawk jumps onto Myeerah's back; White Owl holds her hand. We stagger into the fort just as the sentries are closing the main gates.

Inside is bedlam.

Colonel Bouquet is shouting, children are screaming. Soldiers are running every which way, dragging cannons behind them. Horses have gathered into a jittery herd, with Pasha in the middle. They mill about, ears back and kicking. Cows bellow and run out of the way of the spooked horses. Flocks of chickens squawk and flap their wings in our faces.

Maybelle and the Merry May!

Dragging the children behind me, I run to the middle of the fort. I pry open the doors of the central storage. Myeerah and her boys are just behind me.

"Aunt Betsy, it's dark in there!" Sarah screams. Little Noah's eyes are bigger than eggs. He grabs my dress and won't let go.

I push the cornpone into Elizabeth's—now Elspeth's—hands. The water jug rolls onto the floor; it's

169

too dark to see where it lands. I push Elspeth and Sarah inside and bolt the door.

"No! No! No!" Noah shouts. Peeling his fingers from my dress is like trying to bend iron. He won't let go. I grasp his wrists tightly and jerk hard, break free. I shoot the bolt, open the door, push Noah, White Owl, and White Hawk inside, hear Elspeth and Sarah screaming, slam the door shut, and re-bolt it.

I run toward the main gate, where sentries block my way. "You must let me out, you must let me out!"

"No one in the fort can leave, Miss Zane," one of them says.

"My horses!" I scream. "You must let me out!"

Just then I hear, "Open the gate—it's Colonel Zane."

The sentries open the gate a fraction. Jonathan, Andrew, Silas, Isaac, Old Sam, and Rachel Johnson all rush in at once behind Eb. Pansy lumbers in, bellowing. Maybelle and the Merry May charge the opening, almost knocking us down.

My horses whinny and buck until they see Pasha. They gallop into the middle of the herd. The three of them stand nose to nose to nose, comforted by one another's scents.

"Oh, Aunt Bessie," I say out loud, "I need comforting, too."

13

The Apron

"Water!" Colonel Bouquet cries out. "Everyone to the river! Fetch water!"

All of us: men, soldiers, women I haven't seen since the ball in the Officers' Mess, grab anything we can find—tankards, buckets, canteens, dishpans, washtubs. We stumble down the steep hill and onto the riverbank. As I fill my containers, I hear the Indians and British soldiers on the Ohio shore—trilling war whoops and the color guard beating drums and playing fifes. A few rifles fire; the bullets plunk into the river, just out of range.

Major Linn said maybe six hundred strong. Canoes, crossing the river!

I want to charge up the hill, but of course I can't—my precious water would spill right out of the buckets. I force myself to climb slowly and steadily, as the sound of rifle fire fills my ears. My eyes already smart from the gunpowder. Bullets ricochet off tree trunks and thud into the earth. War whoops just about freeze my blood.

"Is everyone accounted for?" Eb shouts as our soldiers close the north sally port. "Now, put your vessels down

171

and make as much noise as you can. Make as much noise as four hundred instead of forty-five."

We whoop and holler, beating spoons against each other, bashing barrels with broom handles.

"Betsy, come with me," Johnny says. He takes me up the ladder to his battle station, a loophole just above the north sally port.

After a few shots fired forward and back, I see, through the loophole, three men march up the hill. The man on the right carries the Union Jack, the man on the left carries a white flag. All firing ceases.

The man in the middle speaks up.

"I am Captain John Pratt of the Queen's Rangers, and I wish no harm to come to you and your people here. I wish to give you an opportunity to avoid the profusion of blood which will surely flow if Fort Henry is not immediately surrendered to us. We know you have only a few men and are defended by women and children.

"I promise you in the name of King George, if you give up, everyone will be treated with humanity, but I also warn you that if you do not capitulate, we are a large force and prepared to attack with a strength you cannot understand and, in that circumstance all here will most certainly be killed, as no quarter will be given."

"Give up?" Major John Linn shouts. "Ever heard of Saratoga, Captain?"

The man with the white flag speaks. "I am Ensign John McGillen, a Scot and a man of Christian heart. Our artillery will be here tomorrow along with another fifteen hundred Indians fresh from their victory at Blue Licks, Kentucky. No one wants to see children massacred. Give it up, the Zanes, there's no chance."

I whisper to Johnny, "The Zanes will never give up."

"Go to hell," Eb shouts. He gives a signal, and Stephen Burkham fires a shot that tears right through the British banner.

The three men scurry into the brush. Eb climbs down the ladder to stand in the parade ground.

"Silas," Eb says, "I'm putting you in charge of the fort, you and Colonel Bouquet. You and you," my brother says pointing to two soldiers, "will get two buckets of water each, a barrel of hardtack for food, and join me in the blockhouse. We have to guard the ammunition. We make a run for it now."

"This is what my brother's been waiting for," I say to Johnny. "A chance to strut and command."

Johnny grins back at me. Then: "Have you ever cleaned and primed a rifle, Betsy?"

I shake my head.

"It's not difficult. Just make sure you've got plenty of water to cool down the barrel."

"Just show me how, Johnny."

Johnny and I look out our loophole at the wave of Indians and Queen's Rangers charging up our hill. "Haven't fired yet, Betsy, but I will. You'd best get that water."

We are like cogs in a wheel, Johnny and I. All day and far into the evening, every time he shoots one of his muskets,

I wipe the barrel down with water to cool it. He has taught me how to charge anew the flintlocks, and how to wrap the bullets in little squares of cloth. Without cloth, the spark would have nothing to burn, so the gunpowder wouldn't explode. Shoot, cool, reload, shoot, cool, reload. We scarcely say a word to each other.

At sunset Rachel Johnson comes around with enough cornbread and beans to give all the loophole defenders supper.

In the full darkness the shots cease. I rush down the ladder to the central storage to comfort the little ones. Myeerah and Isaac are already there. Stephen and Yvonne Bouquet hold fast to their mother's skirts, sobbing.

"Uncle Isaac!" Sarah screams wildly, her arms around his waist. "When will Ma come back?"

"Soon," Isaac says, stroking her hair. Noah and White Owl cling to his legs. "Very soon."

We try to sleep in the Officers' Mess, but Elspeth, Sarah, and Noah stay awake half the night, crying for their mother and trying to wrest a promise from me that I won't lock them up again the next day.

At the first shot at sunrise, Lucille Van Swearingen, Myeerah, Mrs. Bouquet, and I drag all seven children kicking and screaming into the central storage.

I run to my battle station. Johnny is already there and has primed both muskets. A bucket of water stands at the ready. Rachel Johnson comes around with breakfast.

"Good morning, Betsy," Johnny says. "Ready?"

"Ready."

All morning it is the same as yesterday: shoot, cool, reload, shoot, cool, reload. When Rachel Johnson comes around with our dinner, she has a handful of bullets to give me along with the cornbread and beans.

"Where did these bullets come from, Rachel?" I ask.

"Mr. Silas taught me to make them last night, Miss Betsy," she replies. "Old Sam's keeping the forge fire hot."

"Thank you, Rachel," Johnny says gravely. "With your cooking and your bullets, we can hold fast this fort."

Rachel Johnson squares her shoulders. She looks exhausted; the skin under her eyes is all puffy and purply black.

"You're welcome, Lieutenant." She walks proudly to the next loophole with buckets full of food and her apron full of bullets.

Gunsmoke bursts out of Zane House.

"They've taken over our house!" I cry out.

At the loophole next to us Silas takes careful aim and shoots into the southeast corner window. We hear a scream, then nothing more. Lucille Van Swearingen reloads his musket.

The battle has been engaged for two weeks now, and not one of us in Fort Henry has been killed. Every time the enemy slips into Zane House, one of my sharpshooting brothers kills them. Jonathan says that the enemy will never burn Zane House. It provides too good a cover, despite the price they pay for that cover.

I've never felt so hot. I'm so thirsty, I could spit cotton. What with the running up and down the stairs to fetch water, and all the confusion, my hairpins are long gone. My long hair hangs like a woolen shawl around my sweating shoulders, neck, and temples. My dress is filthy.

And yet I keep fighting.

"Have you noticed? We are like cogs in a wheel," I say to Johnny this afternoon. Rachel Johnson has just made her thrice-daily rounds with food and bullets. "The wheel being Fort Henry, the cogs being the one man and one woman at each loophole."

Johnny nods. "We're all in this together."

I have torn Noah's extra shirt into squares to wrap Johnny's bullets in. I tear the squares into smaller pieces, hoping there's enough cloth to spark the gunpowder.

Today, September twelfth, a black man in Shawnee dress walks up the hill carrying a white flag. All shooting stops.

"The Zanes, and Colonel Henry Bouquet!" he shouts. "Show yourselves!"

Jonathan and Colonel Bouquet step out of the main gate.

"I'm Jonathan Zane. Who are you?" my brother asks loudly. "Who's your master? Did you get lost in the woods?"

The black man stands taller. "I am Pompey, my *own* master. I'm as free as you are."

"You weren't born that way," Jonathan replies, louder still. "You're a traitor! You're a runaway slave who's up and joined with the Shawnee."

Pompey says, "This is your last chance to surrender. We've got two hundred and sixty warriors and forty Queen's Rangers who have vowed to kill every last one of you if you don't surrender at once."

"You tell your British officers and the chiefs," Jonathan says, loud enough for all to hear, "that as long as even one person here has strength enough to pull a trigger, we'll keep right on fighting. Tell them as well that the next time you or anyone else comes walking up here, flag or no flag, he'll be shot dead in his tracks. Now get!"

Pompey turns around slowly and walks down the hill. Jonathan and Colonel Bouquet come back inside.

I leave my battle station, as do Silas and Andrew, to hear their talk.

"Now I've seen everything," my brother says, shaking his head. "A runaway slave Shawnee warrior."

"He said two hundred and sixty warriors," Colonel Bouquet says. "That means the so-called fifteen hundred warriors from the battle of Blue Licks, Kentucky, never showed their faces here."

"He did say that," Jonathan replies, his eyes wide. "I didn't notice any new artillery, either."

"We might win this yet," Silas shouts, pounding Jonathan on the back.

"Not without gunpowder," Colonel Bouquet says grimly. "We've got enough for today—if they don't charge the fort again."

"There's plenty of powder in the blockhouse," Silas says. "Eb will give us however much we need."

Eb and two soldiers have been defending the block-house for sixteen days now.

"But someone will have to fetch it," Silas says. "I'll need a volunteer."

"I'll go," a soldier cries out.

"No, I'll go," another soldier shouts. "I was the fastest runner back home in Tarrytown."

I hear myself saying, "You can't spare the men, Silas. I'll go."

"Betsy," he says with a smile, "I admire your courage, but it's out of the question."

"No, it isn't."

I grab an empty sack and tie it around my head. "Silas, look, now they can't grasp at my hair."

"And just how do you think you'll carry a barrel of gunpowder back with you?" Jonathan asks.

"My apron! It's only forty yards to the blockhouse."

He says, "Your apron! And what are you going to do when you come back? Bake us a pie? Silas is right, it's out of the question, Betsy." Jonathan stands in my way, as does Andrew.

Without stopping to think, I run around my brothers. I open the main gate before anyone can stop me, dart through, and close it softly behind me.

What were once Zane corn and wheat fields with a lush treeline in the distance are now the ruins of a battlefield. Bloody and flyblown, the bloated bodies of Indians and British soldiers lie every which way. The treeline is nothing but blackened, burnt stumps.

Betsy, force yourself to walk slowly, as though you haven't a care in the world, as though you're some empty-headed female who's gone out to pick daisies on a summer afternoon.

Great-Aunt Elizabeth was right. We live in a heartlessly cruel world. Here's your chance to make it less so.

Out of the corner of my eye I see warriors peeping from behind the stumps. "Squaw, squaw," some of them shout. I hear laughter and jeers. But no gunshots ring out, no arrows slice through the air.

I measure my steps, one for each loved one whose life is at stake: *This step is for Isaac . . . this one for Jonathan . . . this one for Silas . . . this one is for Andrew . . . this one is for Eb. This step is for Aunt Bessie . . . this one for Elspeth . . . for Sarah . . . for Noah. This step is for Johnny . . . for Old Sam . . . for Rachel . . . for White Hawk . . . for White Owl . . . for Myeerah. This one is for Maybelle, and this the Merry May. . . .*

I gulp. There are so many more steps!

Slowly . . . slowly . . . This one is for Old Bess . . . for Young Sam . . . for Sarah Peabody . . . for Jane Raffles . . . this step is for Abigail Levy . . . this one for Belinda Weymouth . . . for Herr Dr. Weyberg . . . for Mary Crofter and Mr. and Mrs. Crofter. . . .

By the time I have named every step for everyone and everything in my life—even Pansy, our milk cow, and the Van Swearingen hens, Burgoyne and Cornwallis—I have reached the blockhouse. Slowly, I open the door and face Eb and the two soldiers.

"Betsy, what on earth?" Eb whispers. His face is blackened by grime and gunsmoke.

"We're out of gunpowder. I've come for more," I say, forcing myself to sound more confident than I feel.

179

"Silas sent you?" Eb asks in amazement.

"No one sent me. I volunteered."

"Betsy, I can't let you go back out there."

"Not you, too! You have to let me go. If you send out a man, the Indians and British will shoot him."

"Let her go," a soldier says.

"This is my sister!" Eb shouts back.

"Keep your voice down," I whisper, flinging my apron to the floor. "Pour the powder into this."

"*I'll* make the run," Eb says. He empties a keg of gunpowder into my apron and ties the cloth together at the top. A bit of gunpowder seeps out at the sides.

"I need more cloth," he says to one of the soldiers. "What have you got?"

Eb's hands are full, so the soldier gives me an old sack. I hold out the sack and Eb drops my apron into it. This time, the gunpowder stays put. Quickly, I tie the apron sashes around my waist again.

"I said I'll make the run," Eb says.

"No, you won't."

"Betsy, I forbid you—"

I take a deep breath. "I'm ready. Wish me luck."

I fling open the door.

"Betsy, no!"

Run!

Holding my bulging apron in my arms, I dash for Fort Henry's main gate amid more laughter and shouts of "Squaw! Squaw!"

Then I hear, "Powder! She's got gunpowder!"

180

I run faster.

Bullets rip through the air. I hold my head down and hunch my shoulders. I jump, dodge, and run from side to side, just as a doe does when trying to shake loose a pack of wolves.

Arrows slice through the air over my head. More bullets, this time close to my chin. The gunpowder is heavy, slowing me down.

My heels pound the blackened earth. I jump over a Queen's Ranger, long dead, just as a bullet thuds into his still chest.

The gate, the gate—just a few more steps!

Out of the corner of my eye, I see warriors running toward me from either side. Gunfire. They both fall.

Silas and Jonathan are half hidden at the gate. Jonathan reaches out, grasps my hand, and pulls me forward. Heels up, I crash to the ground. The gate shuts behind me.

I did it!

I roll over onto my back. Faces look down at me— Isaac, Jonathan, Silas, Andrew, Johnny, Colonel Bouquet. My apron full of gunpowder is safe in my arms.

"Betsy," Johnny says, "what on earth?"

"We needed gunpowder," I gasp, "to keep fighting."

"The risk!" Johnny shouts angrily. "What were you thinking?"

"We're all in this together," I reply, panting. "That's what you said."

"I'll be at the loophole," he say scornfully. "You stay

down here where it's safe." He runs up the ladder to his battle station.

"Betsy, are you all right?" Jonathan asks, helping me to my feet. "I can't believe you'd do something so foolish."

"One of us should have gone in your stead," Andrew scolds.

My heart is racing. Sweat is pouring off my forehead. I've never felt this way before—I could run through a hundred battles!

"I did it!" I shout triumphantly.

Four brothers are glaring at me, shock and anger on all their faces. They remind me of the day I came home to Zane Station. Full of outrage, with no thought to my bravery, all they could do was criticize my actions.

"Remember? The day I came home?" I scowl at them, still panting hard. "That took courage! All the way through the Cumberland, to come home! None of you even said hello."

My brothers say nothing.

Colonel Bouquet stands in front of me and clicks his heels. "Young lady," he says solemnly, "for your fearlessness in battle, for your heroism, I salute you."

Then he does.

"Why—why, thank you, Colonel Bouquet," I stammer, too surprised to say anything else.

"Young lady, if we might have our gunpowder," Colonel Bouquet says solemnly. "We have a battle to engage."

"Of course," I say, untying my apron. As I give it to

Colonel Bouquet, a horde of soldiers and settlers clusters round him, a look of relief and good cheer on all their faces.

I glare at my brothers. "I am going to join Johnny at our loophole."

"You heard him, Betsy," Andrew replies coldly. "The lieutenant said he doesn't want you up there."

I don't even bother to answer.

14

October Roses

The Battle of Fort Henry ended on September twelfth, just one month ago today. Once word got out that we had a fresh supply of gunpowder, the enemy gave up and left in the night.

October is the best month for riding. Johnny on Pasha and I on the Merry May ride the river trail every afternoon. What leaves remain on the trees are fiery jewels. The sour gums, buckeyes, and oaks turn yellow, then orange, then flaming red, and finally claret. Lemon-yellow maples light up the deep recesses of the woods. I can see into the forests for miles and miles in all directions.

My view is especially fine, because I still ride ahead of Johnny, to forestall his testy objections regarding Indians and ladylike behavior. As we ride, I think about us in the years to come—Johnny hectoring me as to the proper accouterments and trappings of a lady, and me behaving as one.

When the battle ceased, Eb sent for Pastor William Kennicott Townsend, who came all the way from Pittsburgh to perform Isaac and Myeerah's wedding. Eb said they needed a proper wedding, which raised Isaac's ruff. Later Isaac said it was Myeerah who talked him into it.

I remember our mother's wedding dress, cut from heavy Chinese silk and the color of buttercream, locked in a trunk upstairs. The wedding gown feels like cool water as I help Myeerah slide it over her head. It fits as though it had been made just for her.

Isaac has taught her to say "I do," and "I will," and when to say them.

Isaac is uncomfortable in borrowed clothes. All through the wedding, he keeps tugging at his collar. Myeerah looks lovely in my mother's dress, a sheaf of dried timothy for a bouquet.

I'll wear that dress on my own wedding day. Someday.

Isaac and Myeerah are married in front of our hearth. As the pastor speechifies, I admire the vase full of the very last of this year's roses, sitting in pride of place on our mantelpiece. The scent of roses fills the house.

Who would have thought that a rosebush could be strong enough to survive the Battle of Fort Henry? That rose lady back in Pittsburgh spoke truly when she said roses only look delicate; they're as hale and hearty as weeds. In a week or two, Aunt Bessie and I will prune the rosebush down to stalks no bigger around than our thumbs. The bush will look half dead, but it will grow back even more robust next spring.

Women are like roses, I think with a start. We only look delicate. When my life was pruned down to the very quick, when our only chance was the gunpowder, did I grow, too? Hale and hearty?

I reckon.

Myeerah and Isaac look so happy.

After the wedding we all sit down to a wedding feast. There are platters of hickory-smoked venison, apple puddings, cornpones, stewed papaws, custards, and game stews.

Eb, Silas, Andrew, and Jonathan give toast after toast to the newly wedded couple.

"This is the last of your applejack, Jonathan," I call out.

"I'll make more. We've had a bumper crop this year. Even allowing for all the apples the enemy ate, there's plenty left."

Isaac stands up, raises his tankard, and says, "There wouldn't be a wedding today if it weren't for our Betsy. By making that mad dash to the blockhouse for the gunpowder, she saved Fort Henry. She saved the Zanes. May people remember her bravery for generations."

I reply in my very best taunting manner: "What nonsense! The only reason I made the mad dash, as you call it, was precisely because my brothers and Johnny forbade it."

I hear many a grumble, groan, and protestation from round the table, Johnny protesting the loudest. But I turn a deaf ear to their squawks: Inside I am shining, shining just as brightly as the sun.

Isaac says, "You may think that now, Betsy, but in the years to come, you'll change your mind."

I look at Isaac and see the frank approval in his eyes. He reaches across the table and shakes my hand. "You're a Zane," he says, with a catch in his voice.

"Thank you, Isaac," I say, "thank you very much."

Afterword

With the exception of the Crofters, the rose lady, and Betsy Zane's Philadelphia neighbors and girlfriends, everyone in *Betsy Zane, the Rose of Fort Henry,* was a real person, including all five of the Elizabeth Zanes—Great-Aunt Elizabeth Zane, Betsy Zane, the freed slave Elizabeth Zane Porter, Ebenezer's wife Elizabeth (Aunt Bessie Zane), and their daughter, Elizabeth (Elspeth) Zane.

PHILADELPHIA DURING THE REVOLUTIONARY WAR

In the late eighteenth century Philadelphia was the second-largest English-speaking city on earth—London being the largest. In the square mile between Delaware and Eighth, between Vine Street and Lombard Street, there were some 35,000 people and about 7,000 buildings in the Philadelphia of 1777. Many more people lived in the small towns and crossroads that made up the outskirts of Philadelphia.

Perhaps 35,000 to 45,000 people doesn't seem like many citizens—there are millions of Philadelphians now—but can we even imagine what it must have been like in Betsy Zane's day? People threw their garbage into the streets, and there were no garbage trucks to pick it up. City aldermen allowed pigs to run free, the idea being that the pigs would eat the garbage. Pigs were branded to prove ownership, just as cattle are today.

One thousand horses were stabled in that same square mile, along with chickens, sheep, and family milk cows. There was no indoor plumbing; tossing the contents of the chamber pots out into the street was part of the morning routine.

Philadelphia in the summer is a humid 90–95 degrees. In those days there were few sidewalks. People sank to their knees in human and animal filth. Epidemics of yellow fever and scarlet fever raged through the city every year. The squares that William Penn had so carefully laid out for city parks were more often used for cemeteries.

During the Revolutionary War thousands upon thousands of soldiers died in hospitals set up along the Delaware River. They were buried in what are now Washington, Franklin, Jefferson, and Logan Squares.

It's no wonder that anyone who could afford it built a country house along the Delaware or Schuylkill River. The Binghams, the MacPhearsons, the Logans—even the Penns—lived as far away from William Penn's "holy city" as possible.

On the plus side, thanks to an invention of Dr. Benjamin Franklin's, Philadelphia was the first city in history to have streetlights. Dr. Franklin also organized a volunteer fire department, a public library, and the American Philosophical Society.

Colonial Philadelphia was a haven for Germans who were not members of the Lutheran Church—German Jews, German Catholics, the German Reformed Church, the Amish, the Mennonites. Old First Church on Fourth and Race Streets used to be the German Reformed Church.

There was a Zane Street between Seventh and Eighth

Streets in Philadelphia when Betsy Zane lived there. The Zane Street Grammar School for Girls existed for twenty years, from 1841 until the beginning of the Civil War, when it was closed and reopened as a soldiers' hospital. Since then Zane Street has had its name changed many times. After being known as Zane Street, Sugar Alley, and Elder Street, it became part of Filbert Street in the early twentieth century.

The Pennsylvania Abolition Act

The Pennsylvania Abolition Act of 1780 granted freedom to anyone born to a free woman during and after that year. One of the last slaves born in Pennsylvania was a girl named Haney, born to a slave woman in Chester County in 1811. By then the abolition law had been changed to emancipate anyone on his or her twenty-eighth birthday. Haney was owned by Colonel Thomas Bull of East Nantmeal Township, Chester County, until 1839.

The Zanes

Betsy Zane's parents, Nathaniel and Anna Zane, were living in Moorefield, (West) Virginia, when their only daughter, Betsy, was born. That same summer they moved to what is now Wheeling, West Virginia, and called the settlement Zane Station. Betsy spent her early childhood at Zane Station before moving to Philadelphia after the death of her parents. She attended a Quaker school there and lived with her great-aunt, Miss Elizabeth Zane.

Why were the Zanes Virginians, and not West Virginians?

The people of western Virginia decided to stay in the Union prior to the Civil War. West Virginia became a state in 1863.

Sixty yards from Zane House was Fort Henry. Betsy Zane really did save Fort Henry in September 1782, in the last battle of the American Revolution, just as it is described in this novel.

She married John McGlaughlin when she was still only fourteen. They had five daughters. After John McGlaughlin died, she married Alfred Jacob Clark. They had one son.

She was living in the river town of Martins Ferry, Ohio, when she died in 1823, at the age of fifty-four. She is buried in Walnut Grove Cemetery in Martins Ferry. Her marker reads: *Elizabeth Zane, Heroine of Fort Henry.*

Betsy Zane's granddaughter, Elizabeth Zane McCurry; her brothers Jonathan Zane and Ebenezer Zane; her sister-in-law Elizabeth (Aunt Bessie); and lots of other Zane relations are also buried in Walnut Grove Cemetery.

The Elizabeth Zane Memorial, erected in honor of her heroism, stands at the entrance to Walnut Grove Cemetery. At the top of the memorial is a statue of a girl, her hair tied up in a cloth sack, and with a very determined look on her face. A bulging sack is held tightly in her hands. The memorial reads:

Elizabeth Zane
Whose Heroic Deeds
Saved Fort Henry in 1782
Erected by the schoolchildren of Martins Ferry
May 30th, 1928

The Zanes, the Martins, the Clarks, and the Browns were the first pioneer families to cross the Ohio River in 1785, and to live in what was then known as the Northwest Territory. The city of Zanesville, the first capital of Ohio, was founded by the Zanes. As an adult Betsy was a scout in her own right, leading pioneers from the Ohio River and north through the Zane Trace to Zanesville.

The tiny village of Zanesfield, Ohio, was named after Isaac Zane, who lived in northwestern Ohio with his Wyandot princess wife, Myeerah. Both Isaac and Myeerah died in 1816 and are buried in Zanesville.

The Northwest Territory Charter was granted as an Act of Congress in 1787. The Charter forbade slavery in the lands that would become Ohio, Indiana, Illinois, Michigan, and Wisconsin. Old Sam and his Virginia wife, Rachel Johnson, crossed the Ohio River with the Zanes in the spring of 1785. They were granted their freedom two years later. During the Battle of Fort Henry Rachel Johnson cooked and served all the food consumed in the fort and made all the bullets. She died in 1847 at the age of one hundred eleven.

Betsy Zane's great-great-nephew Zane Grey (1872(?)–1939) was an unsuccessful dentist in Greenwich Village, New York City, who dreamed of being a writer. His first novel, *Betty Zane* (which is how she's known in the Zane family), is about his great-great-aunt and was published in 1915. He wrote dozens of short stories and eighty pulp fiction books about the American West.

None of the Zanes, living or dead, can sort out where they came from. Some claim Denmark. Others say England, then Ireland, then France, before immigrating to America. A Mariposa, California, Zane claimed the family was from Venice, Italy.

In the introduction to *Betty Zane* Zane Grey wrote of a Danish aristocrat named Zane who was forced out of Denmark and settled in Philadelphia with William Penn. Another source says this Danish Zane was in Philadelphia as early as 1677. Apparently, Karl Zane was so arrogant and stiff-necked that he was forced out of Philadelphia as well. Most of the family moved to Moorefield, (West) Virginia.

Scots Coal Miners

Scots coal miners were bound, which is a polite way of saying enslaved, until the mid-1800s. Typical miners (including children) worked up to eighteen hours a day in mines with no safety standards. The families of those killed in the mines were forced out of their homes if they could not pay rent. There was no money for injured miners, nor were there pensions for those too old to work.

Most miners could neither read nor write; the mine owners discouraged education for the "bad effect on profits." Often the only time a miner saw daylight was on Sunday, when the mines were closed. Just as Mr. Crofter did, miners wore iron collars that marked them as bound to the owner of the coal mine. These collars were so hard to remove that miners were often buried wearing them.

LEWIS WETZEL

Lewis Wetzel may have been the worst serial killer in American history. Historians believe he was responsible for the murders of at least 105 Native Americans. He would go into the woods to hunt Indians just as other men would hunt animals.

Lewis was placed in jail repeatedly for his murders and, in 1788, was almost hanged for the killing of a Seneca warrior named Tegunteh, whom everyone called George Washington because of his loyalty to the United States. Lewis Wetzel escaped as he was being led to the scaffold.

In the summer of 1791 Lewis Wetzel was living along the Mississippi River, counterfeiting Spanish money. He spent five and a half years in solitary confinement in a French New Orleans prison for his crime. When he was released, he spent the rest of his life as a trapper—and murderer—living alone along the Ohio and Mississippi Rivers. In 1811, Lewis Wetzel was hunting in the wilderness west of the Mississippi River and was never seen or heard of again.

Wetzel County, West Virginia, was named after the Wetzel family.

Crawford County, Ohio, was named after Colonel William Crawford, who was killed just as Jonathan Zane described.

Aunt Bessie's one-armed brother, Major Samuel McCullough, died just as Silas Zane described it. Major McCullough did take part in the Gnadenhutten Campaign.

Sources

Butterfield, Willshire. "An Historical Account of the Expedition Against Sandusky Under William Crawford in 1782; with Biographical Sketches, Personal Reminiscences, and Descriptions of Interesting Localities, including Details of the Disastrous Retreat, the Barbarities of the Savages, and the Awful Death of Colonel Crawford by Torture." Cincinnati, Ohio: The Ohio Historical Society, 1873.

Doddridge, Joseph. "Notes, on the Settlement and Indian Wars, of the Western Parts of Virginia and Pennsylvania, from the Year 1763 until the Year 1783, inclusive. Together with a View of the State of Society and Manners of the First Settlers of the Western Country." Wellsburg, (West) Virginia: The West Virginia Historical Society, 1824.

Eckert, Allan W. *That Dark and Bloody River: Chronicles of the Ohio River Valley.* New York: Bantam Books, 1995.

———. *The Frontiersmen: A Narrative.* Boston: Little, Brown and Company, 1967.

Garrison, Webb B. *A Treasury of Ohio Tales.* Nashville, Tenn.: Rutledge Hill Press, 1989.

Grey, Zane. *Betty Zane.* New York: Grosset and Dunlap, 1915; reprint New York: Harper & Row, 1992.

The Historical Society of Pennsylvania, 1300 Locust Street, Philadelphia, Pennsylvania 19107.

Ingeborg, MacHaffie S., and Margaret A. Nielsen. *Of Danish Ways.* Minneapolis, Minn.: Dillon Press, 1976.

Kelley, Joseph J. *Life and Times in Colonial Philadelphia.* Harrisburg, Pa.: Stackpole Books, 1973.

Kiracofe, Roderick, and Mary Elizabeth Johnson. *The American Quilt: A History of Cloth and Comfort, 1750–1950.* New York: Clarkson N. Potter, 1993.

Lubin, Isador, and Helen Everett. *The British Coal Dilemma.* New York: Macmillan, 1927.

MacLeish, William H. "From Sea to Shining Sea: 1492," *Smithsonian,* November 1991, pp. 34–48.

Morgan, Shirley O., MFH, the Chagrin Valley Hunt. *Between the Ears: A Unique View of the World.* Fredericksburg, Va.: Bookcrafters, 1995.

Nash, Gary, and Jean R. Soderlund. *Freedom by Degrees: Emancipation in Pennsylvania and Its Aftermath.* New York: Oxford University Press, 1991.

The Ohio Historical Society, 1982 Velma Avenue, Columbus, Ohio 43211.

Rothmann, Sarah Lynde, Information Officer, Royal Danish Embassy, 3200 Whitehaven Street NW, Washington, D.C. 20008-3683.

The Zane Papers, Martins Ferry Public Library, 20 James Wright Place, Martins Ferry, Ohio 43935.